The Midnight Eye Files

THE AMULET

WILLIAM MEIKLE

The Midnight Eye Files: The Amulet

Cover Art by Christian Guldager
www.chrisguldager.com

Gryphonwood Press
www.gryphonwoodpress.com

Printed in the United States of America

To Kent Holloway, a fellow traveler, for all the work that goes unseen, but is appreciated nonetheless.

Gryphonwood Books by William Meikle

The Midnight Eye Files

The Amulet

The Sirens

The Skin Game

The Watchers

The Coming of the King

The Battle for the Throne

Culloden

Stand-Alone Works

Berserker

Island Life

The Valley

Concordances of the Red Serpent

Foreword

I read widely, both in the crime and horror genres, but my crime fiction in particular keeps returning to older, pulpier, bases.

My series character, Glasgow PI Derek Adams, is a Bogart and Chandler fan, and it is the movies and Americana of the '40s that I find a lot of my inspiration for him, rather than in the modern procedural.

That, and the old city, are the two main drivers for the Midnight Eye stories.

When I was a lad, back in the early 1960s, we lived in a town 20 miles south of Glasgow, and it was an adventure to the big city when I went with my family on shopping trips. Back then the city was a Victorian giant going slowly to seed.

It is often said that the British Empire was built in Glasgow on the banks of the river Clyde. Back when I was young, the shipyards were still going strong, and the city centre itself still held on to some of its past glories.

It was a warren of tall sandstone buildings and narrow streets, with Edwardian trams still running through them. The big stores still had pneumatic delivery systems for billing, every man wore a hat, collar and tie, and steam trains ran into grand vaulted railway stations filled with smoke.

To a young boy from the sticks it seemed like a grand place. It was only later that I learned about the knife gangs that terrorized the dance halls, and the serial killer, Bible John, who frequented the same dance floors, quoting scripture as he lured teenage girls to a violent end.

Fast forward fifteen years, and I was at University in the city, and getting an education into the real heart of the place. I learned about bars, and religious divides. Glasgow is split along tribal royalties. Back in the Victorian era, shiploads of Irishmen came to Glasgow for work. The protestants went to one side of the city, the Catholics to the other. There they set up homes... and football teams.

Now these teams are the biggest sporting giants in Scotland, two behemoths that attract bigots like bees to honey. As a student I soon learned how to avoid giving away my religion in bars, and which ones to stay out of on match days.

Also by the time I was a student, a lot of the tall sandstone buildings had been pulled down to make way for tower blocks. Back then they were the new shiny future, taking the people out of the Victorian ghettos and into the present day.

Fast forward to the present day and there are all new ghettos. The tower blocks are ruled by drug gangs and pimps. Meanwhile there have been many attempts to gentrify the city centre, with designer shops being built in old warehouses, with docklands developments building expensive apartments where sailors used to get services from hard faced girls, and with shiny, trendy bars full of glossy expensively dressed bankers.

And underneath it all, the old Glasgow still lies, slumbering, a dreaming god waiting for the stars to be right again.

Derek Adams, The Midnight Eye, knows the ways of the old city. And, if truth be told, he prefers them to the new.

Derek has literary antecedents - occult detectives who may seem to use the trappings of crime solvers, but get involved in the supernatural. William Hjortsberg's Falling Angel (the book that led to the movie Angel Heart) is a fine example, an expert blending of gumshoe and deviltry that is one of my favorite books. Likewise, in the movies, we have cops facing a demon in Denzel Washington's Fallen that plays like a police procedural taken to a very dark place.

But I think it's the people that influence me most. Everybody in Scotland's got stories to tell, and once you get them going, you can't stop them. I love chatting to people, (usually in pubs) and finding out the -weird- shit they've experienced. Derek is mainly based on a bloke I met years ago in a bar in Partick, and quite a few of the characters that turn up and talk too much in my books can be found in real life in bars in Glasgow, Edinburgh and St Andrews.

One

The day started like any other. I dressed, I smoked two cigarettes and I sat in my empty flat, waiting for the phone to ring.

I felt bored. I hadn't had a case for more than a month, and that had been someone looking for a lost cat. I had sat through hours of stories of gangs of kids stealing cats to sell to far-eastern clothing manufacturers, of Chinese take-away shops with bulging freezers, and even weirder tales of devil worship and ritual kitten slaying. I still hadn't found the damned cat.

At least the view from the window kept me distracted. Students walked along Byres Road, hand in hand, oblivious to the world around them. Old bedraggled men waited for the pubs to open, little old ladies in heavy woolen coats carried bags of shopping that were too heavy for them, and old Joe from downstairs continued to sing "Just one Cornetto" at the top of his voice every ten minutes. At ten-thirty I went through to the office, opened the desk drawer, took out the whisky bottle and prepared for the long slide down to bedtime.

Just another lonely day in paradise.

An hour later I eyed the last of my whisky, wondering how long I would be able to spin it out when the knock came on the door. I almost dropped the bottle getting it back in the drawer and just had time to tighten up my tie before the door opened and all other thoughts were swept away.

She was more than beautiful, she was awesome.

I could see that from the cut of her clothes, the way she carried herself, the way her deep black hair was oh-so-carefully tousled. I tried not to stare at her legs as she walked across the office. Her stiletto heels clacked on the hardwood floor as she walked towards me, and I tried, almost successfully, to raise my eyes from her legs.

"Adams? Mr. Derek Adams?" she asked, and her voice sounded just right.

The dream of the Bogart case began to take shape. I stood to shake her hand, noticing how cool hers felt, how sweaty mine had suddenly become.

"That's right. Adams Detective Agency—ADA for short. First name in the book, first when it comes to providing personal service."

I was rambling. I closed my mouth—maybe that way she wouldn't see me dribbling. I motioned her to the threadbare chair in front of my desk and sat down in my own, hoping that, just this once, I could pull off the air of studied nonchalance I'd practiced in the mirror.

"You're not first in the book anymore," she said. "I've already tried 'Abracadabra—we can do magic'. It's in a warehouse over in Maryhill. There's a little man in an office even more ramshackle than this one. I think I intimidated him, though. He turned me down."

She smiled at me and I guessed that a dentist had been paid a lot of money for all that sleek whiteness.

"I know who you mean. Jimmy Allen. He was upset when my entry went in the book above his," I said.

"Maybe it's time you became 'Aardvark Associates'," she said, and laughed.

Something warm and interesting nestled in my stomach.

"No. I'd get more car breakdowns and alcoholics than cases."

She settled herself in the chair, making herself comfortable. I hoped she might stay for a while.

"So what can I do for you?" I asked.

I sat back in the chair and watched her talk—it wasn't hard work.

"We had a burglary two nights ago," she started. "My husband doesn't know about it yet—he's out of the country. The thief knew what he was looking for, and only one piece of jewelry was taken—a most valuable piece. It was a wedding present from my husband and it has great sentimental value. I want you to get it back for me."

Her mouth worked beautifully, but she hadn't told the whole truth. I'd seen it in her eyes as she spoke.

My bullshit detector was working overtime, but it was a fairly standard request; I had handled such work before. Besides, she could lie to me all she wanted—I could handle it for a while.

"You realize how little chance we have of recovering a piece of jewelry?" I asked, trying not to notice the expanse of thigh that became visible as she shifted in the seat.

"I don't think you'll have much trouble with this one," she said. "It's a very distinctive piece."

She dug around in her handbag—which on its own would pay my rent for months—and removed a photograph that she passed over the table. I picked up the picture, and almost dropped it straight away. Suddenly I didn't want anything to do with this, I didn't want this woman in my office, and the whisky in the drawer was screaming to be let out.

Then she smiled at me, and I turned the picture over.

It was a pendant, but unlike anything I'd ever seen before. It consisted of a figurine on a heavy gold chain. There was nothing in the picture to indicate size, but it looked big. Big and ugly. The figure was of an animal, but not any known to me. The hindquarters were feline and striped, like a Bengal Tiger, but from the waist up it looked grotesque, an amorphous blob of black stone with long suckered tentacles streaming from a spherical blob that could have been the head.

"Nice wedding present," I said as I put the photograph down. "If it was mine I think I would be quite glad to lose it."

I pushed the photograph away from me, turning it face down on the table, and rubbed my fingers on my tie, but I couldn't get rid of a feeling of being dirtied by having touched the thing.

"You wouldn't want to lose it if you knew it was worth half a million pounds," she said, and I sat back hard in my chair. "It is very old—Ancient Arabian, I think. Arthur is very fond of it and he'd be very upset if he knew it was gone. That's why I'd like you to find it before he gets back."

I still wasn't getting the whole truth, but I had the scent of money in my nostrils and my dream of the big case in my head.

"I cost £250 a day, plus expenses. Two days in advance," I said, then wished I'd asked for more when she agreed instantly and, taking a book from her bag, wrote me a check.

"Just keep a record of those expenses," she said as she handed it to me. "My husband and I like to pay attention to the details." She smiled again, as if at a private joke.

"I've got an up-to-date book-keeping system," I said, lying and thinking about the old typewriter in the back of the cupboard. "You'll have itemized bills down to the last penny."

She looked round at the cupboard, and back at me.

"Computerized, is it?" she said, and this time the smile was full force. Somehow she knew about the typewriter. I could see it in her eyes.

"Oh yes," I said, digging an ever deeper hole for myself. "All mod cons, Internet link to the tax office and the VAT man, automatic production of bills, there's nothing that little baby won't do."

"And I bet you don't have to change the ribbon more than twice a year," she said.

I let that lie. I was confused enough already without adding another layer of intrigue. Besides, mind reading wasn't one of my specialized subjects.

"Tell me more about the burglary," I said. I took a cigarette from the pack beside me, and she took one when I offered. As I leant over the desk to light hers I got a heady whiff of her perfume—strong, musky, and as sexy as hell. I tried to pay attention as she spoke.

"As I said, it was two nights ago. I got back from the theatre at just after midnight."

"You were alone?" I asked.

"Yes," she replied.

"Shame," I said, before my brain had time to catch up with my mouth. That got me another smile, but she tapped on the wedding band on her left hand.

"Do you want to know about the burglary, or would you rather flirt with me?"

"Is that a trick question?" I said, then settled back in my chair with a sigh. "No, go on. I have a rule against mixing business with pleasure anyway."

"Shame," she said, and gave me a smile that would have melted a glacier.

"Touché. Please go on," I said. I tried to blow a nonchalant smoke ring, ended up getting smoke in my eye, and spent the next minute or so squinting at her. At least she had the good grace not to laugh.

"As I said, I got back after midnight. At first I didn't notice anything untoward, but then I found that the kitchen door had been forced. I did a quick search of the house, and that was when I found that the amulet was the only thing missing."

"You have other valuables?"

"Oh yes. Arthur is something of a collector, and we have many other pieces of equal, if not greater, value."

"And the amulet was all that was taken?"

She nodded.

Something still didn't feel right. It wasn't the stealing on demand that was wrong—that happened all the time. She was lying about something else, and I couldn't pin it down.

"And what about the police?"

"I would rather handle this discreetly," she said. "If the police were involved, Arthur would get to know, and I'm hoping that you can recover the piece without that kind of fuss."

And there was the lie—it was in her eyes, and the tightening at the corners of her mouth. I let her have it for now. My guess was that the husband knew already, but that there was something inherently dodgy about the amulet that precluded official police involvement.

"Insurance?" I asked, and she shook her head, strengthening my hunch.

"Well, as I said already, I don't want to get your hopes up," I said. "I'll do the rounds and ask around. And I may have to visit your house at some point. But you should start preparing your excuses for your husband—we may never find it."

"Just do your best, Mr. Adams," she said. "Who knows? It might be sitting in some high class antique dealers rooms even now, just waiting for you to walk past and see it."

The way she said it made it seem like she was dropping a hint, giving me a clue. But when I looked in her eyes all I got was a small smile.

"Okay," I said. "I'll start straight away. Do you have a number I can get you on?"

She got up and put a business card on my desk beside the photograph and my advance check. With one last smile she left, taking most, but not all, of her perfume with her. I realized that I didn't know her name.

The card didn't yield any clue either—"A&F Dunlop, Dealers in Antiquities", and a posh address out in the suburbs. I assumed "A" was for Arthur, her husband, but "F", "F" could be for anything. I resolved to ask her the next time I talked to her.

I resisted the urge to play with the check and put it away in my wallet alongside her card and a lonely £10 note. The photograph went into my jacket pocket and I went to work for the first time in a month.

Old Joe at the tobacconist on the corner had my two packs of Marlboro ready for me before I even got to the counter.

"I saw your visitor this morning," he said to me by way of a hello.

"Aye," I replied. "She'll keep me in fags for a while."

"She could keep me for as long as she wanted. She was a stunner, was she not? I don't know what she wanted, but I know what she needs," the old man said, and made an obscene gesture with his thumb and forefinger.

"You should be ashamed of yourself," I said, but laughed anyway. "A man of your age."

"Oh, there's still lead in the auld pencil," Joe said. "And when I take my teeth oot, I can still give them a good gumming."

"Away and don't be so disgusting," I said.

He waggled the top plate of his false teeth at me until I laughed again.

"Seriously, though," he said, "I've seen her before somewhere. I can't remember where though."

"Well if it comes back to you, let me know."

He charged me nearly thirty pence more than the day before for my two packs. That in itself was enough to make me think it was time to give up again. But my new client smoked, and I wanted to appear sociable with her, didn't I? I lit a new one from the butt of the old as I left the shop and made my way across Byres Road.

My first stop was Glasgow University. I didn't have far to go. Five minutes' walk and nearly twenty years of my life, that was all. The mock-gothic buildings still loomed ominously over me, just like they did all those years ago, and, for maybe the thousandth time since then, I wondered if I'd made the right decision when I turned my back on it all.

Then, as I made my way down gloomy corridors and stairs to the dark sub-basement where the smartest of my contemporaries worked, I realized, for maybe the thousandth time, why I'd done it.

Doug Lang and I went back a long way. We had been boozing buddies together when we were students and kept in touch, even after I dropped out.

"Still sifting the rubble, are we?" I said as I pushed open the door to his tiny, windowless, room.

He looked much as he had all those years ago—the unkempt hair, the John Lennon specs and the ill-fitting cardigans, all part of the his eccentric professor persona, but beneath it all was one of the sharpest, most inquisitive minds I knew. And, best of all, he was an archaeologist.

"One day somebody like me will be looking through some debris and find bits of you in there. Now won't that be something," he said.

"It certainly would," I said. "I've got myself down for cremation."

He laughed, and it was as if the years had fallen off him.

"It's good to see you," he said. "Have you come to take me for a pint?"

"I'm afraid not." I said. "Business this time."

His eyebrows almost raised through his hairline when I showed him the photograph and he got visibly excited.

"The Johnson Amulet," he whispered, and I thought he would drool over the picture.

"You know it, then?" I asked.

"Oh yes," he said, and lapsed into what I had come to know as his 'teaching' voice.

"It was found in Ur, sometime around the turn of the last century, and was brought back into the country by James Johnson, a shipping magnate of the time. It's got a long history—something about Devil worship or black magic, ancient immortal Arab sorcerers—hocus-pocus, anyway. It caused quite a stir in the twenties. There was some sort of scandal, and Johnson died in suspicious circumstances. The amulet wasn't amongst his effects, and hasn't been seen since."

A predatory look came to his eyes. "Where did you get the picture?" he asked.

"From a client. I've been hired to find it."

He laughed. "Better people than you have tried," he said.

"Is it worth much?" I asked, hoping that I might at least expose one of Mrs. Dunlop's lies, but I was to be disappointed.

"It's priceless," Doug said, and this time I believe he did drool. "Archaeologists the world over would be cutting off parts of their body for just a look at it. I suppose that if it ever came up for auction it would go for, say, a couple of million. But, as I said, it has been lost for around eighty years—some rich private hoarder probably sits and gloats over it during the long winter nights."

"It can't be too far lost," I said. "This picture is a lot more recent than that."

I watched the excitement grow in Doug's eyes. I knew it was time to leave—he was getting close to his manic puppy dog phase, and I would have him following me everywhere if I wasn't careful.

"If I find it I'll let you have a fondle before I give it back," I said

"Come on, Derek," he said. "Let me go with you on this one."

"No way," I said. "Remember the last time?"

Doug had badgered me for months about 'running' a case with me. I'd been stupid, and let him come with me as I tried to track down a missing teenager. When we found the kid in the garden of the parent's holiday home he'd thrown up all over the body.

"That was different," Doug said, pleading. "I've got the expertise this time."

"I'll give you that," I said. "But I really don't want you on the street with me. People will think I'm giving out charity."

"Cheap shot, Derek," he said. "And stop avoiding the subject."

"I'm not," I said. "I've got a bad feeling about this one, and you'll be more help to me here, with the 'expertise' in hand. Besides, the University pays you to do your stuff in here—not out on the streets."

That did it—he backed down—I knew he would when I played on his sense of duty. I turned toward the door, but he stopped me.

"Wait," he said. "You'll be wanting more information about the amulet. I've got a book about it somewhere."

I laughed, and he joined me. It was an old joke between us—there were few topics under the sun that Doug didn't have a book on. The key word was somewhere. Until he got round to marrying a librarian, the chances of him ever finding a book he wanted were slim.

"No," he said. "I know where this one is." He dug into a pile of books behind his desk and came up with a small, dusty, leather bound tome.

"In Ur with a Philanthropist," he read from the spine. "By George Dunlop."

I almost dropped the photograph at the mention of the name, but managed to hide my surprise while putting it back into my wallet. Doug hadn't noticed, and continued.

"Dunlop was well known around here. He was Professor of Antiquities at the University. He did some solid work in Turkey before the Ur expedition. There's some detail about how the amulet was found. More hocus-pocus, I'm afraid. Old Dunlop obviously got too much of the sun out in the desert. But at least you'll know more about what you're looking for."

I took the book from him. It fit snugly into my jacket pocket, and its weight reassured me that I'd at least made a start on the case. I thanked Doug, and left him with my promise of first look at the pendant.

I made my way back to the real world. It was raining again—heavy pelting, driving rain that forced its way through my coat and my trousers.

By the time I got to the bank I'd got wet through even though the walk had been less than a quarter of a mile. The teller smiled at me as I made my deposit, both things rare occurrences.

When I came out of the bank the rain still drove hard, almost vertically along the road. Little old ladies forced themselves into the wind, umbrellas raised in lethal poses. A couple of teenagers passed wearing only thin shirts and light trousers. They thought they looked tough, but the misery in their eyes just made me want to laugh in their faces.

Tennant's bar beckoned as I passed. I knew I had a lot of legwork ahead of me, but the thought of doing more of it in this weather didn't appeal much. The idea of a beer or two loomed large in my mind, but I knew that way led to oblivion. And besides, Doug was right—I did need to know more about the pendant.

I went back to the flat.

I live on the first floor of a Victorian building, shops below, students above. I have my own stairwell, with a security-locked door at street level. During the day I tend to leave the bottom door closed and unlocked, but as I approached I noticed that the door was partially open. It was at times like these that I wished I lived somewhere else, somewhere quieter, where I didn't run the risk of meeting muggers, drug-addicts, or just plain old-fashioned drunks.

There was no one on the stairs, though, just a faint, rancid odor that I couldn't quite place, which faded as I went up the stairs.

My office, or more properly, the place where I receive my clients, is actually a large hallway at the top of the stairs, with my flat proper through a doorway off to the left, and my bathroom to the right.

For furniture I have two large chairs and a desk. They sit in the middle of the large room, and give the place a menacing air, like something out of Kafka. In an attempt to make it more inviting I'd imported a few large pot plants, but they had begun to die on me recently, their browning leaves dotted around on the hardwood floor. Not for the first time I made a mental note to employ a cleaner—a cheap cleaner.

Ten minutes later I went through to the flat proper. I had locked the downstairs door, and was soon settled in my armchair, cigarettes and beer at handy arm's length. It wasn't long before I was lost in Dunlop's world of sun, desert and blinding heat. At some point I drifted to sleep, but the story kept unfolding even then.

We had been in the desert for nigh on two months before things came to a head. Johnson was becoming increasingly discontent with our lack of progress.

"You promised me discoveries," he said to me. "Wonders to rival Tutankhamun or Troy, you said. And what have we got? Clay pots and meaningless daubs on tablets, that's all."

"But we are getting close," I told him, for perhaps the fifth time that week. "Those 'meaningless daubs' you refer to are actually an inventory, a list of the treasures buried with the priest-kings."

"So you've said," Johnson replied. "But where are the tombs? Where are your precious priest-kings? When will you give me anything other than clay?"

And in truth, I couldn't answer him. The tablets spoke of great wealth, but what I needed was a map. And without it, we were digging blind. The tablets and pottery showed we were in the right general location, but it could be months yet before we found anything of value, never mind the tombs of the priest-kings.

That wasn't what Johnson wanted to hear.

"Back in Glasgow, when I asked you the most probable site for us to make a discovery, you gave me this one," he said. His blue eyes were wide and staring, and I feared an outburst at any moment. "Was I wrong to put my faith in you?"

"No," I replied. "It's just that these things take time. Each level must be catalogued and described before moving on."

"Why?" Johnson said, and this time he was shouting. "Just get that bloody dynamite out and we'll blast this dune to hell."

"We can't do that," I said, and it was my turn to shout. "Think of the archaeology."

"Bugger the archaeology," Johnson said, and lifting a clay tablet from the desk he smashed it against my chair. "I need results. And I need them now."

He stormed out of the tent, leaving me to pick up the fragments of tablet. Luckily it had only broken in two pieces, and would be easily matched together. Whether I could reconcile Johnson's needs with those of science was another matter, but I had chosen my bedfellow for the money he could provide to fund the dig. It would be churlish for me to start complaining now.

This had been a dream of mine for more years than I cared to remember. Schliemann had his Troy, Carter had Egypt. I would have Ur, farther back in time than either—the true cradle of civilization. For years I'd been looking for a sponsor. I'd trodden the halls of academe, I'd given lectures to the Royal Society—I'd even talked to women's groups. And it all came to nothing.

Until one night I was at a dinner party in Kelvinside. I was introduced to a big man with blazing eyes and a lot of money. Johnson had caught my enthusiasm, but he wanted gold sarcophagi, facemasks, statues—he wanted to out-do Carter. As for me, I wanted to see the priest-kings, to touch them and know they really existed. I wanted to know how they lived, these people who defined the beginning of our civilization.

I went back to trying to translate the tablets I had been working on before Johnson had stormed into my tent. If I'm being honest, I was almost as frustrated as my benefactor. This had been the hottest, dustiest, most unrewarding dig I had ever had the displeasure to manage. Even Carthage hadn't been this bad. But there was nothing for it but to keep going, keep cataloguing. The scientific method, and the needs of archaeology, demanded it. That didn't mean I had not prayed every night for a breakthrough.

But that night wasn't the one. The tablets for the day spoke of grain, wine and honeycombs. All very interesting, but nothing that would please Johnson. I dragged myself off to my cot and prayed once more for a find.

The next day dawned hot and dusty, just like the sixty days before it. I broke my fast on the tough, dry bread of the area and a glass of lukewarm tea before heading out to survey the progress of the dig.

We were already fifty feet into the side of the dune, and the amount of shoring required to stop it falling on us was increasing all the time. I spent the first hour of the day supervising the next layer of planks before taking myself down to the floor of the dig. Young Campbell had found another hoard of tablets, and he thought these ones were promising. The fact that he'd said the same thing about the last three piles of tablets he'd discovered didn't seem to dim his enthusiasm. I got on my knees beside him and helped to clear the area. I lost myself in the monotony of it, and only noticed the passing of time when the sun came over the cutting and our shadows fell dark on the ground we were working on.

I patted young Campbell on the shoulder.

"Come on, lad," I said. "Time for a break and some water."

And that's when it happened, the thing that changed the dig, and my life, for evermore.

We had just come out of the cutting when a new shadow fell on us. I looked up, squinting against the sun, to see someone walking over the dune towards us.

At first all I could make out was an amorphous shape, like some great jellyfish, and I believe I actually stepped backward in fear as a sudden chill ran the length of my body. But young Campbell was right behind me, and by the time I regained my composure the figure had come out of the sun, and I was able to make out that it was an old Arab, his robes flowing around him.

As he got closer I saw that he wasn't just old, he was ancient. His skin was wrinkled and stained like the bark of an old tree, and his hair hung in loose grey wisps over a liver-spotted scalp. But his eyes were blue, bright and clear, and when he spoke his voice was strong, and his English impeccable.

"I'm looking for Mr. Johnson," he said, as if he'd just met us on a busy thoroughfare. "If you'd kindly direct me to him?"

"I'm Johnson," a voice said to my left. I turned to face my benefactor. It was obvious that the man had been drinking heavily—his eyes were bloodshot and sunk deep beneath his brows. His hair, usually perfectly groomed, stood out at angles from his head, and his skin had a grey, unhealthy pallor. The old Arab didn't seem perturbed.

"Mr. Johnson," he said. "It is a pleasure to make your acquaintance. I believe I have some information for you that will prove to be of our mutual benefit."

Johnson looked at me and raised his eyebrows. I merely shrugged—I had no idea where this man had come from.

The Arab saw the hesitation. He reached into his robes and produced a bottle.

"I have some fine brandy, the sun is over the yard-arm, and your tent will be cooler than out here," he said. "And I promise you, I have an offer that will cure all your problems."

The last was said directly to Johnson, and I saw something shift in the big man's eyes—something that looked like hope.

The Arab took Johnson by the arm and led him off, straight to the correct tent. That was when my suspicions were first raised.

Young Campbell looked at me, and again I shrugged.

"The last thing he needs is more drink," I said, "But if it keeps him off my back, then let him have it. And talking of drink, I need that water now."

Ten minutes later we were back at the cutting. Johnson hadn't emerged from his tent, and there was still no sign of him some three hours later when Campbell and I called it a day.

It was not until nearly sundown that I saw him again. I was on my second cigar, and third gin. The temperature had started to fall, the flies had stopped swarming, and I had changed into a clean suit of crisp linen. Life was almost bearable for a short while. Then Johnson walked past my tent.

He had the distracted air of a man deep in thought, and would have kept on walking if I hadn't hailed him. His hair was back to its usual sleek glory, and his eyes were clear again. Whatever he had spent the afternoon doing, I doubted if there had been any alcohol involved.

"Oh, hello Dunlop," he said, as if it was a surprise to him that I should be in my own tent."I was just taking the air."

I invited him inside and offered him a drink and a cigar. He took the cigar, but turned down the gin.

"I'm afraid I over-indulged myself last night," he said sheepishly, "Trying to drown my sorrows—all I did was give them a swim."

I laughed, but his eyes stayed serious.

"And what about the old Arab? Did he have anything for you?" I asked.

I saw him take some time deliberating on his answer.

"No. Just another desert chancer trying to make some money from the rich foreigners," he said, but he wasn't a good liar.

"And don't worry about last night's row," he said to me. "I'm sure the finds will come in time."

He turned and left, and I went to find young Campbell.

The lad was in his tent, still poring over some of the day's tablets.

"I believe we're getting closer," he said as I entered. "This tablet tells of numbers of servants buried with a great king, and details their families and their worth."

That was very good news, but I was more worried about Johnson's behavior.

"Leave that alone for a minute," I said. "I want you to go and check on the munitions."

"It's Johnson, isn't it?" he said. "He's been talking of little else these past few days."

I nodded.

"He'll know I suspect something if he sees me going near the dynamite. Just make sure that the explosives are out of harm's way and come back straight away," I said. "I'm going to have a long talk with him in the morning. We may need his money, but we don't need it that much."

Campbell dropped a mock-military salute and left.

While he was gone I checked the tablet he was working on. The lad had been right. This was proof that we were in the vicinity of an important burial. I felt my heart beat just a little bit faster as I read on.

And that's when the blast tore through the night air. I almost fell from the shock of it, and was on my way out towards the cutting before the ringing had left my ears.

I found Campbell on the ground close to where we'd been working that day. He was carrying an oil lantern that spluttered and almost went out as I lifted it from his hand, then strengthened again as I bent to check on him. There was an egg-sized bruise just above his ear, but he was breathing steadily, although out cold.

Inside the cutting, sand and dust began to settle. I could just see that the blast had ripped a hole in the dig, a deep yawning blackness that stretched down and into the depths of the dune.

I was torn between helping the lad and following Johnson into the hole. I'd actually chosen to stay with the lad when his eyelids fluttered and he looked up at me. He grabbed my arm, tight.

"You must stop him," he whispered, his voice throaty. He'll destroy the site."

He tried to stand, but dizziness forced him back to his knees. He pushed me away from him.

"Go, and please stop him. I'll be all right."

I didn't need any more prompting. I went down into the dune.

My lantern was barely strong enough to pierce the dust that still hung ahead of me, but there were two sets of footprints on the floor of the passageway. By crouching and holding the lantern close to the ground I was able to follow them downwards.

After ten yards the dust was less dense in the air. I was able to see that the walls to either side of me were no longer just compacted sand; they were stone blocks. We had been close.

Part of me wanted to tarry, to pore over the pictographs that covered the walls, but the sound of a deep chanting from below forced me to carry on downwards. The air got colder, and increasingly more stale and musty. And still the chanting got louder. A chill ran up my spine, and I don't think it was from the cold.

I woke with a start, knocking my ashtray over onto the carpet. It was just after 11:00 p.m. and the room sat in pitch darkness. I rose from the chair, and bent to lift the ashtray. And that's when the creaky floorboard in my bedroom groaned as someone stepped on it.

I stood still, but the noise wasn't repeated. I stepped over to the door and put my hand on the handle...just as it turned from the other side.

I stopped and held my breath.

From far away I heard chanting, a guttural drone that shook through my body as if I stood too close to a bass speaker at a concert. The brass handle went cold in my palm, and when I did finally breathe mist formed in the air ahead of me.

Thud! Something heavy struck the door, then another, shaking the wood in its frame.

"I've called the police," I shouted, realizing even as I said it how lame it sounded.

The door shook once more.

All went silent.

The door handle suddenly felt warm, and I knew, I don't know how, that the room beyond was empty. I turned the handle and stepped inside.

I almost gagged at the stench. My nose told me that something had died, and not too recently, but by the time I reached the window the smell had already faded.

A quick visual tour of the room told me what I knew—it was empty. I tried to open the window, and found it to be locked from the inside. I didn't know whether to be happy about that or not. After I opened it I stood at the open window and gulped air until my heart slowed.

By the time I stepped back into the living room, I had almost written the experience off as a waking dream brought about by my night's reading.

Almost, but not enough to allow me to go back into the bedroom.

I filled a glass with whisky, lit a cigarette, and went back to Dunlop's story. To start with, I had one ear on any noise, and when a car alarm went off outside I must have jumped nearly a foot. But the story had me gripped, and it wasn't long until it took me away once more.

The chanting got louder still, and part of me wanted to turn and flee, to get back to my tent and my gin. But the thought of what might await, and what damage Johnson might do before we could catalogue it properly, drove me onwards. I rounded a corner and found myself confronted with a nightmare.

A sarcophagus had been thrown to the floor, its contents broken and strewn across a wide space. I groaned when I saw the bones mingled with the remnants of clothing and binding—a priceless artifact had already been destroyed.

Johnson was on his knees, holding something small and misshapen in front of him, as if in supplication. The old Arab stood above him, his arms flung wide as he sang his chants into the echoing chamber.

Echoes and shadows ran in the space of their own accord. Statues of great serpents writhed in a crude semblance of life. I felt that if I only once averted my eyes, then dark things would pounce on me and devour me utterly.

The chanting got more strident, deeper and resonant. The thing in Johnson's hands began to glow, at first dimly, like a luminescent moss. Then the light flared between his fingers, so much that I could see his bones through them. The light grew steadily brighter until the sickly green glow it cast was stronger than that of my lantern. Its baleful glare filled the room.

The Arab took the thing from Johnson, and it was then I noticed it was an amulet, a figurine hanging on a heavy gold chain. The Arab pulled the chain over his head, letting the amulet lie on his chest. Once more he raised his arms. He shouted, just one word, and the very air seemed to darken around him. For a second it seemed that he grew swollen and distended. Snakes seemed to writhe in the shadows cast round him, but when he dropped his arms, he was only an old Arab.

The Arab looked around the room and smiled. His expression was one of triumph. He smiled, nodded, and handed the amulet back to Johnson. As he brushed past me on his way out my skin crawled at his touch, as if I had been in contact with evil incarnate. He merely smiled a crooked-toothed grin at me, a smile that never reached his eyes.

"Well, Dunlop, we have our treasure," Johnson said.

I fought down an urge to punch the man, and hurried to the rest of the sarcophagi. There was much to preserve before the desert air did its work.

The phone rang, and I jumped. The book dropped to the floor and I soaked my left leg with spilt whisky.

It was my client.

"Mrs. Dunlop. Is something wrong?" I asked.

"I wondered if you had made any progress," she said. This time I didn't need to see her eyes—I heard the lie. She wanted to ask me something else entirely, and my clients were not in the habit of calling me after midnight. I started to pay attention. This case had depths I hadn't started to fathom.

"I've been doing some background work," I said. "I'll know more tomorrow."

"And everything is okay?" she asked. "Nothing out of the ordinary?"

Strangely I thought of the typewriter in my office. She had known of that.

Did she also know about the presence that I had felt in the bedroom?

"No," I said, then a thought struck me. "But if any ancient Arab sorcerers turn up I'll be sure to let you know."

There was a sharp intake of breath at the other end of the line.

"Tread carefully, Mr. Adams. We'll do what we can to help you, but we're relying on you to find the amulet for us."

"We," I said. "You and Mr. Dunlop?"

She cleared her throat.

"Yes. Arthur is here. I couldn't lie to him, and I told him about the burglary."

Another lie. She was storing them up.

"I'll phone you tomorrow," I said.

"I'll look forward to it," she said, and hung up on me.

After that the book didn't appeal. I turned on the television and watched a very old hospital drama while smoking cigarettes, drinking whisky, and trying not to think about Mrs. Dunlop. After a while the weeping and wailing from the television forced me to get up to turn it off, and I stood by the window, watching the raindrops find their way down the glass and not seeing the life in the city beyond.

I nearly had a life once. It was back when Doug and I were just getting to know each other, and Liz was still alive.

I was a student—Organic Chemistry and Molecular Biology with a view to majoring in the biochemistry of cancerous cells. I managed to hold down the studies, and had plenty of fun between all the work. Liz and I had met the previous summer…one of those thunderbolt things that blew us both together. We were living together within a week, and had been inseparable ever since. We studied together, discussed our studies together, and partied together.

That all changed during my third year of studies. Although marriage had never been mentioned, we were pretty much a couple, and my old bed was seeing plenty of action. The night my life changed—the 30th of January—started like many others. Doug and I left another dull chemistry lecture and had a few pints in the Student Union. I was several sheets into the wind when I got back to the flat, and that was always a recipe for disaster.

She wanted to talk, I didn't want to listen, and a blazing row ended as it usually did…I slammed the door behind me as I went back to the bar.

I got involved in a darts match against a team from Edinburgh University, and I was having fun, even although I was so bad at the game that I was the one who ended up buying most of the drinks. At some point in the evening the barman called me over and offered me the phone handset.

"It's your girlfriend," he said. "She says she needs you right now."

The drink had spoken for me.

"Tell her she needs her head examined. I'll be back when I'm good and ready."

And so help me, I'd enjoyed myself. While she sat in an empty flat and decided on the future course of our lives, I enjoyed myself. I drank a lot of beer, I sang bawdy songs about the Mayor of Bayswater's daughter—and the hairs on her dickie-die-doh—and only have a vague memory of getting back to the flat.

I'll never forget the next hour, though.

I wandered into the kitchen, bumping into tables and knocking over chairs. That took a minute.

I put on the kettle, and stood beside it while it boiled. That took three minutes.

I took the coffee into the front room and watched the end of the late night news. Ten minutes.

The beer told my bladder it needed to get out. I put down my coffee and got out of the chair—slowly—I wasn't very steady. One minute.

She was in the bath, and she had used my razor on her wrists, her ankles and her throat. She hadn't wanted to make any mistakes. This wasn't a cry for help—she'd tried that earlier and I hadn't answered. For the past fifteen minutes she'd been dying.

By the time the police arrived I was nearly sober, but after they found her note and showed it to me, I got drunk again quickly. She had been three months pregnant.

Doug took me in that night. It was he who cleared out the flat and got me somewhere new to live, and it was he I leaned on through the funeral as I tried to avoid the tear-stained eyes of Liz's family. But he couldn't persuade me to stay on in my studies.

The road from there to here was long, and well-traveled. I stood by the window and let self-pity take over, pity for lost opportunities and lost loves. I was still there when the sun started to come up.

It was too early to start hitting the streets. I made some coffee and went back to Dunlop's book. Old Joe had opened up the paper shop downstairs, and it was only a matter of time before the strains of 'Just one Cornetto' wafted my way again. But the coffee revived my spirits, and the book stole my thoughts away again, this time to the Mediterranean and a stifling hot day eighty years before.

It was nearly a fortnight before I saw the old Arab again, and then it was in a place where I never expected him.

Things had been hectic since Johnson's find. Young Campbell and I had worked non-stop; cataloguing sarcophagi, desiccated bodies, and more golden statuary than even Carter had managed. Johnson had somehow magicked up a coterie of journalists, and even the London Times had managed to get a representative on site.

Johnson was desperate to get his 'trophies' back to Glasgow, and some items were being boxed and shipped even as we catalogued them. As I said, we were very busy, so it was some time before I noticed that the amulet I had seen was nowhere on the manifests. It wasn't until we were on the boat and leaving the docks at Alexandria that I managed to catch up with Johnson.

He laughed when I asked for the piece.

"Oh no. Not that one. That's my reward for my patronage, and my promise for the future."

"I'll expose you when we get home," I said, but even as I said it I knew that it was an empty threat. Johnson was not going to worry about the opinions of some old archaeologist. Not when he was going to be front-page news.

Young Campbell was enraged when I told him. I found him pouring over the large collection of gold serpents we had found.

"Professor," he said to me, "I think we have something here. I think there was a serpent cult. Not just that, I think their main god was serpentine."

I had to agree with him. Too much of what we had found pointed in that direction. There was one particularly squamous sculpture with a multitude of snake-like heads that made my skin crawl just to think about it. That thought also brought to mind the shadows that had seemed to follow the old Arab. I told Campbell about my conversation with our sponsor.

"It cannot be allowed," he said, his face flushed. The bruising around his head was only now beginning to fade, but it still lent a yellow cast to his skin. "It clearly says in the contract for the dig that all finds will be the property of the museum."

"Aye," I said. "But what can I do?"

A sly look came over the young man's face.

"Don't worry, Professor," he said. "I think I know what needs to be done."

Would that I had stopped him there, I might have saved him. But if truth be told, I didn't think he would cause any mischief.

I had miscalculated the desire for revenge brought on by the blow to the head.

We spent the next hours going over the manifest and checking that all the boxes were secure before Campbell professed himself tired. He took his leave, and I wandered up to the foredeck to watch the sunset and smoke a last cigar of the day.

There was a slight coolness in the air, a hint of the welcome awaiting us back in Glasgow. I was actually looking forward to a slate-gray sky and endless drizzle. I could think of nothing finer than a walk through Kelvingrove Park in the rain with my lovely wife. It was while I was in this reverie that I heard the first scream.

I dropped the cigar overboard and ran down the inner stairs to the lower decks, taking three at a time.

The screams came from the vicinity of my own cabin, and they rose louder, then suddenly cut off. I turned a corner a bit too sharpish and barreled into a figure coming the other way. We raised our heads at the same time, and I found myself staring into the smiling eyes of the old Arab. He pushed me away and left at a run. I considered following, but it hadn't looked like he was the source of the screams. I turned and headed towards the cabins.

My cabin door was open and Johnson was on his knees beside a body. As I entered he took something from the body's hand and secreted it in his suit jacket pocket. But I had no time to consider that.

Young Campbell was not going to get time to prove his serpent theory.

He lay in a crumpled heap, and his body looked strangely deflated. It was only when I turned him over that I could see the extent of the damage that had been done. He had been eaten.

Eaten by something with a very small bite. A lot of very small bites.

After confirming the lad had passed on, I raised the alarm. The ship was scoured, but no old Arab was ever found.

TWO

I woke, having slept all night upright in the armchair. It took me several seconds to realize that the phone was ringing, and several seconds more to answer it.

"Is this Adams Detective Agency?" a young voice asked. They sounded far away, and their accent was more California than Glasgow.

"Yes " I said, warily…I got my fair share of crank calls.

"I think I'm being followed " the voice said. "And I'd like you to find out who it is."

"You mean you don't know?" I asked.

"No. I sometimes catch a glimpse of him, but they're too good at what they do and I can never catch them at it."

I thought about my caseload. The amulet case was all I had—it wouldn't hurt to take on another.

"Where are you?" I said. "I'll come and have a chat."

"Just off the San Diego turnpike " he said. "It's…."

I stopped him.

"I'm not an American " I said.

"That's okay " he replied. "Nobody's perfect."

I laughed.

"No " I said, "I mean I'm not even based in the US. You've got a number in Glasgow, Scotland."

There was a silence at the other end of the line, then he hung up without saying anything else.

It was to be the start of a day when everything was slightly off-kilter, a day I never got the hang of.

Dunlop's story still resonated in my head an hour later as I made my way to Maryhill. It was obvious that the archaeologist believed that the amulet was in some way involved in Campbell's death—what else could Johnson have put in his pocket? But if a search of the boat hadn't found any old Arab, maybe he had never been there at all? Maybe Doug was right—the old man had caught too much sun out in the desert. All the same, I hadn't taken the picture from my pocket yet, and the thought of just looking at it again made me uneasy.

The walk up Byres Road didn't help any. Besides thinking about Dunlop's book, I just couldn't get Liz, and the past, out of my head. Every shop I passed, every pub, reminded me of that time. The facades might have changed, and students were certainly better dressed now than then, but the mood of the street stayed the same.

Liz had called it "Urban Bohemian". Charity shops and batik specialists, vegetarian cafes and art-house bookshops, you'll find them all in most University towns. It's just that in Glasgow they're concentrated in one street, a street that's shared with bookmakers, drinking men's pubs and off-licenses. The nonacademics and the students share an uneasy existence that sometimes breaks out into acts of sudden violence, but this morning, with the sun shining and the wind only a breeze, all was quiet.

I walked quickly until I reached the Botanic Gardens at the north end of the road, and took the path down to the side of the Kelvin where I stopped and lit a cigarette. I didn't tarry long, though. Liz and I had spent a lot of time in this area, and I'd done enough wallowing for one day. I followed the footpath up into Maryhill.

As I climbed away from Byres Road, the houses became more rundown, and the shops started to sport graffiti and metal shutters. Rubbish lay exposed in thick black plastic bags that had been ripped by dogs, seagulls, desperate drunks and drug-addicts. The faces of the people were more pinched, more pockmarked, and young people loitered in packs, daring me to look at them the wrong way.

Yet even here reminded me of Liz. Where I had seen losers and down-and-outs, she had seen poverty and the downside of the class system. She had nearly brought me round to her way of thinking, but her death had brought my education to a halt.

There, I'd done it. I'd thought about her again.

Maybe wee Jimmy Allen would improve my mood.

I had lied yesterday when I told Mrs. Dunlop about the phone book. Jimmy and I had been playing a game for nearly five years now.

When I started out, it was as 'Adam's Detective Services'. Jimmy was running a 'cat and wife finding' service called 'Allen's Detective Services'. He rang me up to complain that I'd usurped his position in the phone book. We'd met for a drink, got on well together, then I found he had become 'Adams Detection Services'. I countered with 'Adams Detection Outsourcing', and we were off and running.

I'd given up early last year at "Adams Detective Agency", but Jimmy had got the bug. He got fed up explaining to everybody why he was using the name 'Adams', and started working his way down the 'Acs', then the 'Abs'. I noticed as I approached his 'office'—the end block of a Victorian warehouse—that 'Abracadabra—we can do magic' had already been badly painted out and replaced by 'Abacus Detection—let us add it up for you'. I rang his doorbell and waited while he closed down his extensive security systems. Eventually the door opened and his small head poked through as small a gap as he would allow.

"Oh. It's you, Derek. I wondered when I'd see you."

He opened the door to let me in. By the time I had locked the door behind me and turned round he was already halfway across the barn towards his 'office'.

Jimmy wasn't a private detective, or rather, he wasn't just a private detective. He was an antique dealer, a pawnbroker on the grand scale, and, rumor had it, a part-time fence for anything that wouldn't draw too much heat. He had been doing them all for more than fifty years, and his 'collection' had never stopped growing.

Above me in the rafters hung musical instruments, stuffed animals, shop mannequins and fur coats. The floor area was a series of aisles: white goods and televisions to my left, books on shelves along all four walls, modern sofas and chairs to my right, and antique furniture ahead of me. I also knew that there was a hidden cellar where Jimmy kept gold watches, rings, gemstones, and enough diamonds to keep an Amsterdam jeweler happy for decades.

Jimmy himself looked even more bent than usual. A chronic back problem had got worse over the last few years so that he now seemed to be permanently staring at the floor. He must have been in his late eighties, but he hadn't slowed down any. In fact, if you believed him, he still participated in a full and very imaginative sex life.

If that was true, it had more to do with his chat and his easy way of making you laugh than his physical attributes. He was about five-two, and seven stone soaking wet. He had a hooked nose of which an eagle would have been proud, a liver-spotted scalp that resembled a map of the Hebridean Islands, and a grey goatee beard that looked like each hair had been glued on individually. He reminded me of a gnome from one of the Old Norse tales, or a leprechaun that had gone to seed. I laughed at that thought, and the sound echoed around me, causing sympathetic noises from the vibrating instruments overhead.

"What's so funny?" Jimmy called back at me.

"This " I said, waving my arms around. "Your cavern of delights. It's like something from a fairy tale."

"Grimm or Anderson?" he asked.

"Oh, Grimm " I said. "Definitely Grimm."

He laughed this time.

"Rumpelstiltskin?" he said.

"Yep. Where's all the spun gold?"

"Wouldn't you like to know " he said, and laughed again. I don't think I've ever known a man who laughed quite so much.

"Are you coming or not?" he called out at me. "Or will we just stand here and shout at each other a bit?"

As I walked towards his office I noticed that he had come into possession of some new items. A French bedroom set—three-door wardrobe and two huge tallboys—dominated the left side of the aisle. They looked expensive.

Jimmy saw me looking.

"Got it from a City councilor. On his uppers. Needed some quick cash. Something to do with his wife, a prostitute, and a newspaper. I gave him a couple of grand." He cackled that high, almost girl-like giggle that I had come to know so well.

"Anybody I know?" I asked.

"No " he said. "But you will...you will."

"If you get any more stuff you're going to have to get a bigger place " I said.

"No, they'll only take me out of here in a coffin " he said, and laughed. But this time the echo sounded flat and hollow.

"I've got someone coming to take away all the washing machines " he said, "Some kind of artist—he says he's going to make a giant model of a housewife out of them. Says it'll win him the Turner prize."

"The council will probably buy it, and put it on a hill somewhere " I said. "I can see it now—'The cleaner of the north' or some such shit."

The old man cackled again.

"I've bought some Fifties furniture to replace them. And I've managed to get something for you as well " he said. "Something special."

I followed him through the furniture to a cleared square in the center of the warehouse. There were two armchairs, a desk, a fridge, an early Twentieth Century shop till, and a series of large ledgers alongside a pile of other books on the desk. This was Jimmy's 'office'. High-tech, it wasn't, but I'd never known the old man to forget a deal, or, more importantly, the price of one.

"Before you tell me why you've come " he said. "Have a look at this and I'll get you a beer."

He handed me a book and went to the fridge.

It was a first edition Chandler, a first American edition, of The Little Sister. It was in near perfect condition, even the dust-wrapper, and my heart started pounding faster even before I opened it.

"You wee bastard " I said to him as he came back and handed me a very cold can. "You know I'll never afford it. Just showing it to me should be a criminal offence."

He cackled again.

"It's only three grand " he said. "Working for Artie Dunlop, you should be getting that much a day."

I dropped the book in my lap, and I think my jaw fell as well. Jimmy saw my surprise.

"You didn't know who she was?" he asked, and there was genuine astonishment in his eyes. "I spotted her right off, and gave her a body-swerve. I don't want to be getting involved with the likes of him."

I had been blinded, by her, by the money, by the case. Now I'd somehow got embroiled with one of the shadiest, most feared, members of the Glasgow underworld. I took a long gulp of the beer, wishing it were something stronger, and shakily lit a cigarette.

"Aye " Jimmy said, shaking his head. "That Dunlop. Dodgy Art and Antiques a specialty, along with disappearing enemies whose bodies are never found. I hope she's worth it—you always did think more with your balls than your brain."

Artie Dunlop was something of a legend in Glasgow. The police had never pinned anything on him; he had no other known associates, no 'gang'. But somehow, anybody who ever crossed him disappeared, permanently. Artwork and antique thefts of very high value were attributed to him, but there were never any clues linking him to crime scenes. He was feared by even the hardest men in this hard town.

"Christ " I said, and managed a hollow laugh. "I only asked her for two-fifty a day."

Jimmy laughed so long and hard that he brought on a coughing fit.

"Oh boy " he said when he'd finally recovered. "I knew you were naive, but I didn't think you were stupid as well. What's she got you doing?"

"Looking for one of the dodgy antiques " I said, sheepishly. "Somebody else was stupid, and burgled the Dunlop's house. They've lost a trinket. A million pound trinket."

I took the picture from my pocket and showed it to him. He held it for all of two seconds before giving it back to me.

"I'd want it to stay missing. Ugly looking thing, isn't it?"

I agreed.

"No cops?" Jimmy said, and answered it for himself. "No. Dunlop keeps away from them. And you came to see if anybody tried to offload it on me?"

I nodded.

"No " he said. "Way out of my league."

He answered my next question before I asked it.

"I'd try Tommy McIntyre out at Anniesland Cross, or one of the big antique dealers in town. Macey and Johnsons, or Durban and Lamberts. One of them will probably have been approached by now. Unless it was a 'to-order' job. In that case, you've got almost no chance, it'll be in a collectors hands already."

"Aye. I know that " I said. "But I'm getting paid to try."

"Good luck." he said. "But I'll bet you a grand that it has gone already."

"You've got a deal " I said. "I might only be on two-fifty a day, but the chance to take a grand off you can't be turned down."

I chugged the last of my beer and put my cigarette in an ashtray that would have cost a couple of days of my current fee.

"If you hear anything, you'll let me know?" I asked.

"Only if you get me a picture of Mrs. Dunlop in her birthday suit " he said, and cackled again.

"You'll have to get in the queue for that one " I said, and when he laughed, I joined him.

I gave him back the Chandler.

"Can you hold this for me? I might be able to afford it in a couple of years."

He shook his head.

"I've got somebody in mind for it " he said, and gave me a sly smile. "Now away you go and earn your fee. Maybe, if you find what you're looking for, she'll give you a bonus."

"Aye, right " I said. "And maybe I'll get that picture of Mrs. Dunlop for you. The chances are about the same."

As I left I heard his deadbolts and locks fall into place behind me.

"Don't lock yourself in, old man " I shouted.

"Don't worry about me " a muffled voice shouted. "I've got five crates of whisky in the cellar."

His high cackle followed me back down the road.

"Hey, mister " a voice said to my left. "Have you got any spare change?"

I'd stopped just outside the football ground. It was training day for the team and a handful of youngsters hung around, waiting to see the players enter.

"Come on, mister. Give us a pound."

I'd been trying to ignore them, but three kids, none older than twelve, now stood in front of me, trying to look menacing.

"And what do you want the money for?" I asked.

"Fags " one of them said.

"A bottle of cider " another said.

"How about you?" I said to the third one. He was all of four feet tall, but he already had the swagger and cock-sure manner of someone much older.

"I'm going to go down the docks and get a blow job " he said.

He'd made me laugh; I'll give him that. I gave him a pound.

"Here " I said. "But don't forget to ask for your change."

They were already arguing how to split the money as they turned away from me.

I decided to take Jimmy's advice and headed for the town center. There were several antique dealers besides the two he'd mentioned, and I could rattle a few cages by showing the photo around. It looked like it might rain again soon so I caught the bus. I sat upstairs where I could sneak another cigarette. It was just my luck that I got the "nutter". I seemed to attract them.

"Hey. Give us a fag " a voice said. I looked up into a face that hadn't been washed for at least a week.

"Come on, man " he said. "Just one tab. And a light. That'll do. Oh, and maybe a couple of quid for a wee drink if you can spare it."

He sat down beside me, forcing me up against the window. Apart from not shaving, he smelled like washing was just a distant memory.

I let out a big sigh and gave him a cigarette. He took it and put it behind his ear.

"That one's for later. Can I have one for now?" he said. He smiled, and there were more gaps than there were teeth.

"You've got a brass neck, I'll give you that " I said, giving him another. We smoked in silence for a bit before he replied.

"Aye. Pity it's not a brass todger, eh? Sorry missus " he said as a woman two seats in front turned and tutted.

Suddenly he burst into song, a pitch-perfect rendering of 'A Wandering Minstrel, I' from the Mikado. He was impressed that I could fill in the bass harmonies. The woman two seats in front tutted at both of us, but I gave her my evil-twin grin and she turned away.

"Ye ken Mr. Gilbert and Mr. Sullivan?" he said.

"Aye, But only the Mikado, really. I was in the bass line in a production at school " I said. "And I was only there because o' the lassies in the soprano section."

He launched into 'The Lord High Executioner' before I could stop him.

"That's a fine singing voice you've got there " I said when he'd finished.

"Thank you, sir. I wiz trained well. Now about that fiver you promised me?"

I laughed again.

"As I said, a brass neck."

I reached into my jacket to get my wallet and give him some money, and the picture fell out. Before I could stop him he had bent and lifted it.

He took one look at it, and started singing, a strange, discordant hum that sounded almost mechanical. People started to leave the bus, and I would have joined them if he didn't have me boxed in. Beads of sweat formed on his brow, and he seemed to be straining. It looked like he was trying to stop himself singing. His right hand moved slowly over his left wrist, and before I could stop him, he burned himself with his cigarette. Slowly, deliberately, he ground the red-hot tip into his flesh until the singing faltered and stopped.

He turned the photograph face down and handed it back to me carefully. There was no sign of pain on his face.

"Does Mr. Dunlop know you've got that?" he said.

My world suddenly lurched.

"You know what it is?"

"Oh, aye " he said. "I've seen the original."

"And where would that be?" I asked, but he backed away.

"Mr. Dunlop was good tae me " he said. "And I dinnae ken you. Thanks for the smokes."

He was down the stairs and off the bus before I could stop him. When I looked out, I saw him hustling a bus queue.

I wondered how a derelict came to be acquainted with Dunlop, but couldn't see the connection. I put it away to think about later, got off the bus, and hit the streets.

Macey and Johnsons was my first port of call—an antique dealers on West Regent Street. I remember walking past it many time in my student years—there was a second-hand bookshop two doors down where I had bought most of my textbooks—and sold them again when I dropped out. I'd never been inside though—it always looked too rich for my tastes.

A small frontage opened out once you were inside to a large room lined in gilded mirrors and imposing oil paintings. Small pieces of dark furniture were strategically placed around, and expensive-sounding clocks ticked away in the background.

I wasn't given any time to browse—maybe my jeans and trainers marked me as too poor. A sharp-suited salesman was onto me before I had gone five yards.

He was young, younger than me, anyway, and everything about him looked too tight, from his shoes to his small, mean mouth.

"Can I help you, sir?" he said. The way he said 'sir' made me dislike him immediately.

"Which one are you?" I said.

He looked at me blankly.

"Sir?"

"Macey or Johnson?"

"I'm Edward Macey " he said. "But the name above the door belongs to my father."

"Good for him " I said.

This time, when he spoke, he was less officious, more confrontational.

"Can I help you?" he said again.

"I hope so " I said. "I recently won the lottery, and, having bought my new house, I need to furnish it."

He immediately became more attentive. I could see him working out his most expensive items to sell me, and how much commission he would make. I let him dream for a long second, then let him down, hard.

"Unfortunately for you, I've already got all the furniture and paintings. But I am looking for some knickknacks to leave lying around."

His face went purple.

"We don't sell 'knickknacks' sir. We are dealers in quality furnishings."

"Aye " I said, "I can see that. They're nearly as good as the ones I've got already."

By now he was nearly apoplectic.

"If you're not going to buy anything, I'd like you to leave " he said and began to usher me towards the entrance.

"Hold on a minute " I said. "I am in the market for a piece. A 'quality' piece."

He stopped pushing me, but I could see that he was just waiting for the next wind-up. His eyes widened when I showed him the picture.

"This is what I'm after " I said.

He laughed at me.

"Sir is joking again " he said. "It's been a long time missing. And if I had The Johnson Amulet, I would be telling my father where to stuff his job and retiring, not standing here in a too-tight pair of shoes listening to wastrels like you."

He was telling the truth, I saw it in his eyes, and this time when he ushered me towards the door I let him do it.

"So, you're not going to sell me anything, then?" I said.

"I don't think that would be worthwhile. I doubt if you could afford anything in the shop. I doubt if you could even afford my shoes."

"They wouldn't fit me " I said, but he'd already forced me out the door and shut it behind me.

I had a similar response at four more dealers. If any of them had been offered the amulet, they were too good at lying for me to tell. At least I had spread the word that someone was looking for it, but I felt in a foul mood by the time I turned up at Durban and Lamberts.

Theirs was a new shop, in the regenerated Merchant City to the east of the town center. When I was a student, this area had been a soot-blackened warren of crumbling tenements and public houses that only little old men with lost faces ever frequented. Now it was young, bright and thrusting, full of wine bars, Italian clothes shops and places that would sell you a sandwich if you could afford to take out a mortgage. I preferred it when it had a soul.

I'd heard of the antique dealers, of course. It was the store where rock stars and footballers bought the things that defined their lifestyle. They had scored a coup last year when they shipped a Byzantine necklace over to California for the Oscars, and got the latest skinny starlet to wear it. I had never been inside this one, either. It wasn't that it was too rich for me—I just couldn't see myself ever wanting anything that they sold.

It was like walking into a 1970's sci-fi movie. I almost wished I'd brought some sunglasses. The walls were white, a brilliant, scintillating white. There were maybe ten items on display, all on cubical white pedestals, all encased in a pale blue glass that looked like it cost more than the antiques themselves. I stopped and looked at the first one.

It had once been a piece of crystal, almost a foot cubed, glowing in silver, purple and black. An artist, someone with exceptional talent, had carved it into a cathedral, one with its roof open to the skies. Tiny robed figures worshipped around an altar. There was a figure above the altar, something that didn't look quite human, but as I bent for a closer look, I felt a hand on my shoulder pulling me back.

"Fourteenth century, Italian " a deep voice said, "And way too expensive for you."

I turned to face the voice, and had to look up. He was at least six-four, and big with it. There were wrinkles around his eyes, and he was nearly bald. I had him pegged for at least sixty but his eyes were pale blue and clear, and his grip was strong on my collarbone.

He wore a thick gray tweed suit, the kind I always associated with old colonels, heavy brogues, monocles and gun dogs. His shirt was white and pressed to a smooth sheen, and the pin in the center of his Italian silk tie held a stone as big as my little fingernail. I caught a whiff of expensive cologne as I peeled his hand away, having to fight to do it. I knew who this was; I'd seen him on television at the Oscar ceremony.

"Mr. Durban, I presume " I said.

He smiled, but it didn't reach his eyes.

"I've recently won the lottery " I said, "And...."

He stopped me and raised his hand.

"Save me the music hall act " he said. "Your name is Derek Adams, and you're looking for the Johnson Amulet."

Now it was my turn to smile. I nearly managed it.

"You know me?" I said.

"No, but we antique dealers are a close-knit bunch. When somebody does the rounds accusing us of illegal activities, we tend to let each other know."

"Let me guess. Edward Macey?"

"A credit to his father " Durban said.

"His shoes are too small for him " I said, but it didn't raise a smile.

"When you asked him about the amulet, he remembered me. I have somewhat of a passion for the piece " Durban said. "It's been my life-long desire to hold it in my hand."

"And do you have it?" I asked.

"Unfortunately, no. It was very remiss of Mr. Dunlop to lose it, though, and I'm sure he'll pay dearly to see it again."

He had the smile back again, like a cat playing with a mouse. This man was guilty of something, and it looked like he didn't care that I knew.

"So you know where it is?" I asked.

"That's for me to know " he said. "Now I must ask you to leave. There is nothing in this shop that someone in your profession can afford."

"So your circle of dealers keep telling me " I said. "But remember that I'm working for Arthur Dunlop. I may have more money than you think."

"I'd make the most of it " Dunbar said. "I've heard that Mr. Dunlop is very ill. You might find that your fee won't be forthcoming for very much longer."

I nearly told him that my client was actually Mrs. Dunlop, but I decided never to tell this man more than I had to.

"So you have no knowledge at all of the fate of the amulet?"

"None that I would tell you " he said.

So we were even then—neither telling the other anything. There was nothing more to be gained here—not at the moment.

On my way out I nodded towards the crystal cathedral

"It's worth more than a grand, then?" I said.

"More than a million " he replied.

I nodded, and made sure I nudged the blue glass heavily in passing. I enjoyed the sudden look of panic in his eyes as I left the building.

For a time I loitered outside the shop and made a show of taking my time in lighting a cigarette. Durban stood at the window and watched me, a sardonic grin on his face.

He was playing with me. I knew it, and he knew it. I didn't know whether he had the amulet or not, but he certainly knew more about it than anybody else I'd talked to, including the fact it was missing. I walked across the road, took a window seat in the cafe opposite and settled in for a wait.

Durban still stood by the window, but he was no longer looking at me. I saw him take a call on his cellular phone, then he moved away. But unless there was an entrance I didn't know about, he was still in the shop.

I'd already resolved that I would follow Durban when he left. I just hoped he didn't work too late.

A waitress arrived at my shoulder.

"Yes?" she said.

"What happened to 'Can I help you sir?'" I said.

She looked at me as if I was stupid.

"What?" she said.

She moved her gum from side to side. I noticed that she was actually a very pretty girl. Her long black hair hung heavy on her shoulders, her eyes were deep, chocolate brown, and a nametag over her left breast said 'Eileen'.

"What's the other one called " I said.

"Right tit " she said. "Which describes you perfectly."

I liked her.

"I'll have a coffee. Long, black, and none of that latte nonsense."

She actually smiled, and her face lit up. She dropped me a mock salute and moved away.

I smoked another cigarette and watched the world pass outside. It was nearly lunchtime, and office workers were beginning to fill the streets. I almost envied them their sharp suits, their well-organized days. But then I thought of spending my time in a hermetically sealed office, working in a box among tens of other boxes. No, thank you. My life was disorganized, and I liked it that way. Besides, I got to have chance encounters like the one I was about to have with Eileen.

She brought me my coffee, and I noted appreciatively that it was filled to the top of the mug, and piping hot.

I thanked her, she nodded, and was about to turn away when I asked her to stay.

"Do you know the owners of the shop across the road?" I asked.

"What, Mr. Durban?" she said.

"Aye. Any gossip? Any juicy stuff I should know? Does he like wee boys? Or does he eat babies."

She giggled, and I saw the teenager she had been—and not that long ago.

"What are you? A reporter? And is there any money in it for me?"

"I don't have an expense account, if that's what you mean. And I can't get you your picture in the papers."

"Cop?" she asked.

"Private dick " I said in my best Bogart voice, and I got another laugh.

"Come on. Nobody does that. It's just old American television shows, isn't it? What's the matter—did you see too much of The Rockford Files when you were younger?"

"No, really " I said, and showed her the license in my wallet. She wasn't to know that wee Jimmy had got it for me for a tenner. "And I lied a wee bit about the expenses—I might stretch to twenty quid if you know anything I can use."

"I don't know anything. Well, not really " she said. A voice called her name across the room and she turned away again. I caught her by the arm.

"When do you get a break?" I said, and gave her my best smile.

She returned it, but there was a hint of uncertainty there.

"Three o'clock " she said. "I get fifteen minutes."

"I'll be here " I said. "I've got nowhere else to go."

I left the coffee to cool slightly and went to the pay phone, making sure I could still see the entrance to the shop across the road.

First of all, I phoned Jimmy.

"Hello, wee man " I said. "How's tricks?"

"A quiet day " he said. "Although I might have to get the environmental health folk round. I think something's died behind the walls in here. It stinks something terrible."

"Probably a kid that got caught in your security system while trying to break in."

He laughed.

"Chance would be a fine thing. The wee buggers try it at least three times a week. These systems are costing me a fortune."

"Aye " I said. "But think how much you'd lose if they didn't work."

"Don't even mention it " the wee man said. "I have enough trouble sleeping at night as it is."

"I need some gen " I said.

"Always willing' to oblige " he said. "Just remember, I still want that photo."

"Durban " I said. "Of Durban and Lamberts. Is he clean or dirty?"

I got the cackle again.

"Oh, he's dirty enough " Jimmy said. "But nothing too illegal. He's more your 'weekend wizard' out in the stockbroker belt."

"What, witchcraft?" I said, incredulous. "I thought that died out in the sixties."

"Aye. Mostly it did " Jimmy said. "But you know the kind of thing—robes, orgies, altars and the occasional dead cat. You'd think they'd be too old for it, but I know of several pillars of the community that are involved. I just wouldn't like to have to watch it. Who wants to watch old folk having sex?"

This time it was me who laughed.

"And this from the man who was boasting to me about the videos he'd been taking of himself with young lassies."

"That's different " the little man said. "I don't look at myself."

"You're not turning puritan on me, are you?" I said.

"Not while there's still women around like yon Mrs. Dunlop " he replied.

"Just forget about her for a minute. Anything to report on Edward Macey?"

"Nothing " Jimmy said. "He's squeaky clean. His daddy got him the job. I suspect he pulls the wings off flies in the quiet of his own home, but he's too scared of losing his position in society to do anything even slightly dodgy. Now his daddy—he was another story."

"Bent?" I asked.

"As a nine-bob note. He was into everything he could get his hands on."

"Could he be the fence for the amulet?" I said.

"Not unless his health has improved. Last I heard he was in a nursing home in Skelmorlie. He had a stroke—a massive one."

"And there's no chance the boy is involved?"

"Next to none. He's chasing some society blonde—it would queer his pitch if there was anything dodgy going on."

Yet another dead-end. I had to start finding roads that went somewhere.

"Remember the photo " Jimmy said, and hung up on me.

Next I phoned Doug.

"Any joy on the case?" he asked.

"Nothing yet. This town is like the three wise monkeys—nobody's heard, seen, or said anything."

"So, when are we going for a beer?" he said.

"Not until the case is over " I said. "It's getting a bit complicated. Have you still got Internet access at home?"

"Yes. Do you need something?"

"Anything you can get on Arthur or Artie Dunlop."

"The one that's been in the papers? The gangland guy?" he said.

"That's the one " I replied, and another thought came to me. A coincidence that might turn out to be something else entirely.

"And while you're at it, can you cross reference with Gilbert and Sullivan or The Mikado?" I asked.

"Weird shit " Doug said. "What do you hope to find?"

"Anything, nothing, I don't know. I just thought I'd keep you away from the porn for a wee while."

There was an embarrassed silence on the other end of the line before he spoke again.

"Come on, Derek. You know I only use the web for research."

"Oh yeah " I said. "Etruscan strippers, Aztec nudes... that kind of thing? I've heard there's some good sites depicting Babylonian orgies that have great pictures of dusky maidens with big knockers."

He gave me a nervous giggle.

"I could tell you where to find them, but then I'd have to kill you. I'll see what I can do on your query. Ring me tomorrow " he said abruptly, and hung up on me.

I liked being around Doug. It was just too easy to wind him up. I'd have to stop it…sometime when it wasn't quite as much fun.

When I turned away from the phone there was a little old lady waiting behind me.

"Have you finished, son?" she said. "Only I need to phone my boy...he had an appointment with the consultant in the Western General this morning about getting a wee problem with his waterworks sorted out and...."

I stopped her. I knew the type—let her get started and you would be there for twenty minutes or more.

"That's okay, I'm finished " I said.

"Thanks, son " she said. "I just hope it's not one of those new-fangled phones. I can't be doing with all this technology. It was much easier in the old days when..."

"Excuse me " I said, and brushed past her. "My coffee's getting cold."

"Oh, I cannae abide cold coffee " she said. "I remember the time when..."

I turned away from her, but she'd already aimed her conversation at one of the waitresses, and kept going without even breaking flow. It would be some time yet before her son got a phone call—I thought he might be relieved at that.

I spent the rest of the afternoon drinking coffee, smoking cigarettes, and hoping that Durban wouldn't leave the shop until I'd had a chance to speak to Eileen. The clock clicked, painfully slowly, around to three.

I was on my fifth cup of coffee, and feeling over-heated and bloated when Eileen touched my arm and sat down opposite me.

"You're a savior " I said. "Watch the antiques shop. If Durban comes out, give me a shout."

She spoke to me, but I didn't hear. I was already on my way to the washroom. Only another man will understand the blessed relief that visit gave me. I was thankful that she was still looking out across the road when I got back.

"Nothing to report, sir " she said, and gave me another mock salute as I sat down.

"Thanks " I said. "You can stand down."

She reached over and took one of my Marlboros.

"What are these? American?" she asked.

"Yes. They're pretty strong if you're not used to them."

She shrugged and lit up.

"So why all the cloak and dagger?" she asked.

"I'm on a case " I said. "And Durban knows something about it. I'm keeping an eye on him for a while, and anything you can tell me would be useful."

"I don't really know much " she said. "And Mr. Durban's friendly with my boss. I don't want to get into any trouble."

"It's just between you, me and the gatepost " I said, and she looked at me again as if I was stupid. Maybe I was getting old—my patterns of speech didn't seem to register with the young.

"It's just that he's weird " she continued. "And not just him—there's all those old folks he sees every Thursday."

"Every Thursday? Like, two days time Thursday?"

"Well, today's Tuesday, isn't it?" she said, and I got that look again. She was beginning to think I was a bit simple.

"They turn up at the shop after closing time. They must be eighty, if they're a day. There's four or five of them, the women all with fur coats and the men with smart suits. He takes them away in that big flash car of his. One day he brought them in here. They wanted iced tea, cucumber sandwiches, that kind of thing. And they treated the waitresses as if they were servants. Then they left big tips. Weird, huh?"

She was younger than I had first thought, probably no more than nineteen. I suppose I could excuse her some confusion at the foibles of the elderly, or the values of an older era.

"And this happens every Thursday."

"I told you that, didn't I?"

She sucked on her cigarette like a baby with a dummy. She smoked like a beginner, in small puffs, with little being inhaled. I double-breathed a smoke ring to show her how it should be done.

"Neat trick " she said. "But we had an old guy in here last week that could blow rings out of his ears. Now that was impressive."

"I'm sure it was."

I thought better of trying it—it sounded like something you might need an operation to do properly.

"Is there anything else you can tell me about Durban, or his partner."

Her face screwed up in concentration, and suddenly she reminded me of Liz. She shook her head.

"That's it. And I've never seen a partner—only Mr. Durban."

Maybe I should have got Doug to check up on the antique shop for me. There might be something there. I made a mental note to ask him later, then immediately forgot it.

"Well, thanks for your time " I said to the girl. I took a twenty-pound note from my wallet and passed it across the table.

"I get off at six " she said as she took it. "I could let you buy me a drink?"

But Liz was too big in my head. Eileen must have seen something in my eyes. She shrugged and left the table.

"Your loss " she said as she left. "I might not be able to blow smoke rings, but I've got other tricks."

"I'm sure you have, darling " I muttered after her, but she either didn't hear me, or chose to ignore me.

I ordered another coffee, but it was a different waitress who brought it.

Another chance gone. Over the years there had been a few, and each time Liz stopped me doing anything about it. Wee Jimmy was always berating me and trying to goad me with details of his, probably fictitious, sex life. But I just wasn't ready. I might never be ready.

For the next two hours I nursed a cold coffee and watched the shop. I hoped they had a high profit margin on their items, for in all the time I'd sat there, they had only three customers. The lights went out at five-fifteen and Durban left the shop.

I rose and looked around for Eileen, but she wasn't around. I was almost tempted to hang around until six and let the case take care of itself. But I was getting paid, and I'd just feel guilty if I let my personal life interfere—at least so early in the case.

I left the café and followed Durban at a safe distance. He wasn't hard to tail. His height, his bald head, and the distinctive grey suit made him an easy target. I followed along about twenty yards behind until we reached Queen Street station.

He walked straight onto a train and I had a bad moment when I thought I'd lost him, but when I boarded I spotted him further down the carriage. I took a seat where I could watch the back of his head, and settled in.

By the time the train left ten minutes later, it was standing room only. I realized I didn't even know where the train was headed. The conductor helped me out with that, announcing stops at Stirling, Dunblane, Gleneagles, Perth, Dundee, Stonehaven and Aberdeen. When the guard came round to collect tickets I cut my losses and bought a single to Perth. I was pretty sure Durban wouldn't commute any further than that.

I got worried when he didn't disembark at Stirling, but at least the crowd had thinned. When he got out at Dunblane I slipped out a safe distance behind him.

I'd been in the town before, some ten years previously. A train from Dundee broke down, and a group of us had decamped for two hours in the pub opposite the station. That was the limit of my local knowledge. I hoped he didn't live too far from the station—I might have some trouble finding my way back.

By the time we got down to the Station Hotel there was nobody between us, and I had to drop back further as we walked up the High Street towards the Cathedral. It was getting dark, and I almost lost him again when he turned into the driveway of one of the small cottages in the Cathedral Square. I walked past his door, and saw him moving around in the front room, putting on lights and checking his mail. It looked like he was home.

I checked out the area looking for somewhere I could lurk without drawing too much attention to myself. I noticed that there was a pub The Tappit Hen, across the square with outside seats, and decided to mix business with pleasure.

I had to enter the bar to buy a pint, and I got strange looks from the locals as I ran in, ordered a beer, and rushed out with it again. Durban was still in his front room, settled in front of a huge television set. I settled down for a wait.

He kept watching television, and I did the rushing trick in the bar again before, about nine o'clock, he finally moved. A light came on in the garage at the side of the house and he drove a large sliver 1960's Rover out onto his small drive. He parked it outside the house, and my heart sank as he waved across to me.

"Goodnight, Mr. Adams!" I heard him shout. "With all that coffee, and now the beer, you must need some relief, so I thought I'd let you know I'm off to bed now."

His laugh echoed around the square as he went back indoors, and I put my head in my hands. Some detective I turned out to be. I went back to the bar, slowly this time, and ordered another pint. At least the beer was good. The only other good thing to come out of the debacle was that I was now sure that Durban had something to hide.

When I finished my beer I walked over to his car. It was a thing of beauty; a forty-year-old classic in mint condition. The leather on the seats gleamed as new, as did the vast expanse of woodwork on the dashboard. There was a suitcase on the back seat, but I didn't think I'd get away with breaking in to the car to find out what was in it.

I heard the noise of feet on gravel and looked up.

"Can I give you a lift to the station, Mr. Adams?" Durban said from just outside his doorway. "I wouldn't want you to catch a chill on the way home."

"Are you sure you can't tell me anything about the amulet?" I asked. I had to have one more try—he knew I was onto him, so it couldn't hurt.

"As I've said, I have no information that would be of any use to you. Nothing you would understand, anyway " Durban said. "I would go home and get some sleep, Mr. Adams. If you want to find Johnson's amulet you're going to have a busy day tomorrow."

He was enjoying himself, and his laugh followed me as I turned away.

I made my way back to the railway station with my tail firmly between my legs. On my way I passed an off-license. I went in and bought a good bottle of malt and put it on my credit card. It was beginning to look like the case was going nowhere, so I figured I'd make the most of the money while I could.

I had a half-hour wait for the ten-thirty train, and had a hard time fighting off the call of the bottle. Things got worse on the train when the guard wouldn't recompense me for the unused part of my Perth ticket.

"How do I know you haven't been to Perth?" he asked.

"How do any of us know anything?" I asked, but he wasn't in the mood for philosophy. I had to stump up for another single back to Glasgow, on the credit card again.

By the time I got back to Queen Street station, it was raining, and I couldn't get a cab until I'd walked nearly halfway home. It was almost midnight as I paid the cabby and turned towards my door, only to be confronted by two of the people I had least wanted to meet.

"Mr. Adams " the taller, heavier, one said. "Can we have a wee word?"

"It won't take much of your time " the thinner one said.

Of all the people I didn't want to meet, these two were on top of the list. Detective Inspector Hardy, the fat one, and Detective Sergeant Newman, the thin one, "Stan and Ollie" on the street, were cops. Hard-nosed, no-nonsense cops who believed their own publicity. I let them into my office and hoped I wasn't in too much trouble.

I laid my damp jacket over the back of my chair, took the whisky from its box, and offered them a drink.

"No, thanks " Newman said.

"Not while were on duty " Hardy responded.

I shrugged and poured myself a large one. I downed it in one smooth gulp.

"In some parts of the island that would be considered a criminal offence " Hardy said.

"Nearly as bad as putting lemonade in it " said Newman.

Their style of alternating speech was beginning to grate on me.

"So which toes have I stepped on this time?" I asked.

"We need to know your movements " Newman said.

I spoke before Hardy had a chance.

"Well, the toilet's through there " I said, motioning to the door.

"Funny " Hardy said.

"Very " Newman replied.

"I wonder if Mr. Harris is laughing " Hardy said.

"Who's he?" I asked.

I wanted to sit down in the chair, but that would have left them looming over me. They intimidated me enough already without me giving them any more advantage. They were dressed almost identically, in long black woolen coats that reached their ankles over black Italian suits. The only difference was in their shirts, Hardy white, Newman blue. I suspected that they would have worn trilbies if they thought they could get away with it. Their black shoes were buffed to a deep shine. Legend on the street had it that they were steel toe capped, but I wasn't about to rile them enough to find out.

As I said, Hardy was the taller. About six-one, and twenty stone, he was a big chap. He had recently taken to shaving his head, and along with the moustache and small beard, it gave him a menacing, almost psychopathic, look. He pumped iron, and although his stomach had spread in the years that I'd known him, he was still someone I wouldn't like to meet on a dark night.

Newman was his physical opposite. He stood about five-nine, and weighed only nine-stone at most. He wore his hair long at the collar, and affected tinted aviator sunglasses, even at night. His coat seemed to hang off him, and rumor had it he was an evil, vicious sod who would have been in jail if he wasn't a cop.

A further rumor had it that they were partners in bed, but I wasn't about to go down that route.

While I was musing, Hardy had taken out his notebook.

"John Harris. Local derelict and moocher. No fixed abode. Age: thirty-nine. Last known address: a private psychiatric hospital in Ayr. Found dead at eight this evening at the back of Buchanan Street Bus Station. Cause of death: multiple lacerations."

I thought I could see where this was going. I poured myself another drink and lit a cigarette, pleased to note I wasn't shaking.

"Sorry " I said. "I don't know the man."

"Maybe this will refresh your memory " Newman said, and dropped a photograph on the desk.

He was at least ten years younger, and he was clean, and clean-shaven, but I recognized him. It was my singing friend from the bus.

And that's when I made the mistake. Maybe it was the drink talking; maybe I just didn't like having cops in my office after midnight. I lied to them.

"Sorry, again " I said. "I've never seen him before."

I took another sip of whisky as they looked at each other.

"Maybe you'd like to reconsider?" Hardy said.

"It'll look better later when we have to take you in " Newman said.

But I had told the lie. Now it was time to live with it.

"Sorry, guys. Still a blank. But if anything comes to mind I'll be sure to call you."

"Fobbing us off, are you?" Newman said.

"We don't give up that easily " Hardy said.

I sighed deeply and lit a cigarette.

"So why me?" I asked.

"Where were you at eight o'clock tonight?" Hardy countered.

"Out in the sticks." I said. "Having a pint in Dunblane."

"And I suppose you've got an alibi?" Newman said.

I took out the train tickets from my wallet and showed him them.

"Two singles? And one of them to Perth? Any reason why?" Hardy asked. They had moved closer to me, and now all three of us were crowded around the desk.

"It's a long story " I said.

"We've got time " Newman said.

"And two train tickets don't prove you were there " Hardy said. He leaned even closer until we were almost nose-to-nose. "Where were you at ten o'clock?"

"Dunblane station, waiting for a train " I said. I took the credit card receipt for the whisky from my wallet and put it beside the train tickets.

"Haddows off-license, Dunblane High Street, 9:45 " I said, tapping the receipt. "And the barmaid in The Tappit Hen in Dunblane will verify that I left there about half-nine."

"Smart arse " Hardy said.

"A no-friend smart-arse " Newman said.

"Shall we tell him?" Hardy said.

Newman nodded, and Hardy took out his notebook.

"James Henry Allen, 10 Dalgety Mansions, Maryhill. Private detective, antique dealer, pawnbroker, fence and one-time resident of Her Majesty's Prison Barlinnie. Aged eighty-nine. Died 10:30 p.m. Cause of death, multiple lacerations."

"No " I said, almost shouting. "Not wee Jimmy."

"A closed room murder case " Hardy said.

"Very tasty " Newman said.

"Security locks all still in place and alarmed " Hardy said.

"How do you feel now, no-friend smart-arse?" Newman said.

I moved towards him, and he raised his hands, but even when angry I wasn't stupid enough to hit him.

"So why come to me?" I asked, sitting down, hard, in the chair and lighting a new cigarette from the butt of the old.

"We found this on his desk " Hardy said, and took a package from his pocket. It was a plain brown parcel, with string wrapped around it. It was addressed to me, in Wee Jimmy's handwriting, but had no stamp on it. Surprisingly, the cops hadn't opened it.

I turned it over in my hands. I knew exactly what it was. The old man always was soft for the big gesture.

"Are you not going to open it?" Newman said.

"Don't keep us in suspense " Hardy said sarcastically.

"I don't need to open it. I know what it is. It's a book " I said. "An old book of Jimmy's that I admired."

"Something juicy?" Newman said.

"Porn?" Hardy said.

"No " I replied. I suddenly felt old and weary. I wanted these guys out of my life so that I could drink the whisky and remember the old man.

"No " I said again. "It's a real book. No pictures, just words and ideas. You should try reading one sometime."

"I've read one " Hardy said.

"He didn't like it " Newman said.

Their double act was getting on my nerves. I tore open the package and showed them the Chandler. A card fell out of it.

'A very merry unbirthday to you ' it read, and sudden tears came to my eyes as I recognized the old man's handwriting.

"It is a book " Newman said.

"Aye " said Hardy. "And it's not even new. Nothing for us here just now."

"We might need to talk to you again " Newman said to me.

"That's all right " I said, not looking up as they left. "I'm not going anywhere."

I sat there holding the Chandler and drinking whisky until nearly half the bottle was gone and my tears had all dried up. .

I remembered the first time I'd met the old man. All I knew of him before that was the voice at the end of the phone that accused me of stealing his place in the phone book.

I'd arranged to meet him in the bar of The Pond Hotel, and I'd dressed for the part. I had a double-breasted suit, a kipper tie, and a high collared shirt pressed to perfection. Under the jacket I wore a pair of thick black braces, held up, not by metal clamps, but by buttons sewn into the trousers. Nobody would see them, but I knew they were there, an essential part of my detective- noir persona. I smoked a Camel non-filter, and playing with my authentic forties Zippo.

"Let me guess " a voice said. "The Continental Op?"

I looked up, and saw Jimmy for the first time.

"No. Marlowe." I said.

He sat down opposite me.

"Philip or Christopher?"

"How about Lew Harper?" I said.

"No. He'd never be seen dead in that suit. I've got you pegged more as Mike Hammer. You haven't got a big-breasted-blonde assistant who does your typing and breathes deeply a lot have you?"

I shook my head. "But I'm working on it." I said.

"Pity " he said, "I would have forgiven you your transgressions if you had."

He ordered two pink gins, with angostura bitters, and we spent the rest of the night talking about private detectives, both old and new. We agreed about Hammett and Chandler, disagreed about Ross McDonald, The Rockford Files, and Magnum, and agreed we didn't think Bob Mitchum was Marlowe, but that Powers Boothe had been okay.

They had to throw us out at closing time.

After that we shared cases. Or rather, I pumped him for information, he usually provided it, and I sent him all my divorce cases—the more sordid the better.

I'd prepared myself for his death. I knew it wasn't that far away, but I'd been looking for a hospital bedside, or him keeling over in a bar. I'd never even got a chance to say goodbye.

I put the Chandler in my desk drawer. It would be a long time before I got round to reading it. .

By this time the room had gone a bit fuzzy, and my legs betrayed me when I tried to stand. Although it was now past one in the morning, I called my client—if she could call me after midnight, it was the least I could do to return the favor.

To my disgust she answered on the second ring. I didn't even have the satisfaction of getting her out of bed.

"Mrs. Dunlop?" I said. "Mrs. Arthur Dunlop."

"Mr. Adams?"

I heard the question in her voice.

"I can't find your damned amulet, Nanki-poo won't be singing 'A Wandering Minstrel' again, and my best friend is dead. I'm off the case."

I was just about to put the phone down—and I might have managed it if I had been more sober, then she said the words that made me keep listening.

"We'll double your money " she said.

"You know me so well " I said, and noticed I was slurring.

"Mr. Adams, you are drunk " she said.

"Yes ma'am " I said. "And you are a liar, but in the morning I'll be sober."

Give her credit, she actually laughed.

"Churchill was better. Double the money, Mr. Adams " she said, and hung up on me.

"Damn " I said to the handset, "I wanted to do that."

Three

I woke just as the sun came up. I was still sitting in my desk chair, with one leg on the desk and the other on the floor.

My back felt like I had been stretched on a rack, and several small furry things had slept in my mouth. And not just slept either—my mouth felt like it had been used as a toilet. A cold shower, a change of underwear, two cups of coffee, and my last cigarette went some way to making me human.

Old Joe struck up the first 'Just One Cornetto' of the day. That meant the newspapers had been delivered, and he was ready to receive customers.

When I got downstairs, he had my two packs ready for me, but I made him put them back.

"Camels, please Joe. For old time's sake " I said.

"Feeling maudlin?" he asked, but I didn't reply—I was scanning the front pages of the papers. There was no mention of Jimmy, or of the light opera singer John Harris. And I'm sure old Joe hadn't heard either—he'd have mentioned something to me.

"I just fancied a change " I said, taking a Herald and paying him. "Can a man not change his mind?"

"Not after five years. And not as often as a woman " Joe said, and laughed. "And talking about women—I've remembered where I saw that stoater before—the one that visited you a couple of days ago."

I'd been on my way out, but I turned back.

"Don't tell me. Artie Dunlop."

The old man looked shocked.

"She's mixed up with 'The Undertaker'? Then maybe it isn't who I think it is. But I saw her double in Blackpool, in a fortune telling booth. About ten years ago now, but I never forget a pair of legs."

"I don't think so " I said. "She doesn't seem the type." But then I remembered how she seemed to know about the typewriter. Then again, she'd known I was drunk last night as well, but that hadn't been difficult.

I left Joe with the promise that I'd keep him posted. There was little chance of that—the only time you told Joe anything was if you wanted the whole West End to know quickly.

I stepped out of the shop, and found Doug trying to force something through my letterbox.

"I only want it if it's a plain brown envelope stuffed with twenties " I said in his ear. He jumped, suddenly flustered, and spilled a wad of A4 sheets across the pavement.

I helped him pick them up.

"They're all out of sync now " he said accusingly. "I hope you're not in a hurry to find out what I found."

I looked at the pile of papers.

"Christ, Doug. How much is here?"

"Don't worry " he said. "It's not as bad as it looks. There's a lot of repetition—I haven't had time to sort it out yet."

"You weren't up all night, were you?"

He looked sheepish.

"I got carried away " he said. "You know how it is."

Actually, I didn't—I'd so far managed to avoid hooking up to the Internet. I preferred to get my information first-hand, or as near to it as possible.

"I suppose I'd better give you some coffee " I said. "I wouldn't want you falling asleep at your desk—who knows what the world would come to."

I led him up the stairs. He tutted when he saw the whisky bottle. I didn't tell him why I'd been drinking; the wound was too raw. If I started talking about the wee man again, I'd start drinking again. Much as the idea appealed, I had work to do.

"Park your bum " I said and motioned him to the desk. "And tell me what kept you away from the triple-X sites."

"It'll be easier if you read it " he said. "It's a bit far-fetched, and you'll have a lot of questions."

"Okay. I'll do you a deal " I said. "You shuffle them back into the right order, and I'll make the coffee."

When I got back with the coffee there was a neat pile of paper on the desk in front of my chair.

"Fast work " I said. "Have you been practicing your poker shuffle again?"

"It wasn't as bad as it looked " he said.

"What is it about?" I asked.

"Just read it " he said. "You'll be entertained, if nothing else."

I gave him my newspaper, a coffee, and a cigarette, then I settled down to read.

The top pages were all about Arthur Dunlop. There were fuzzy pictures taken with long telephoto lenses, masses of press speculation, hundreds of column inches, and nothing I didn't know already.

"Thanks for this " I said. "But it's all standard stuff. What about the Gilbert and Sullivan link?"

Doug leaned over and sorted the papers before handing them back to me.

"There you go. There's the good stuff."

The heading at the top of the first page read "http://www.moonlichtnicht.co.uk/harris. html."

"What's this—the Harry Lauder appreciation society?"

That one went over his head.

"No, it's a 'magazine of the weird'. One of the sites where conspiracy theorists and UFOlogists gather."

"UFO...what? I said.

"Just read it, will you " Doug said. "I've got to be at work in half an hour." .

It all began on September 20th, 1987. John Harris was a musical prodigy and a Doctor of Physics, a youth with perfect pitch and an interest in the acoustic properties of archaeological sites. He had already, at the age of twenty-four, published several papers that had stood archaeology on its head.

He had made it clear that ancient man had been much more 'acoustically sophisticated' than had been supposed, building their tombs, halls and homes as perfect places in which to sing and play music. His book The Acoustics of the Ancients was already much sought after by those in the know, and he was working on a blockbuster tentatively entitled Did Cheops play Jazz?

with which he intended to prove that the Great Pyramid at Giza was actually a giant acoustic amplifier.

On that day in September, John was studying tablets in the Hunterian Museum in Glasgow University. These tablets had been brought from Ur by the infamous Johnson expedition, and he'd had to get special permission from the University authorities just to look at them. He was working on a new theory—that some of the untranslated tablets actually held an undiscovered form of musical notation.

John hoped that, by gaining knowledge of how the Sumerian's music was structured, he would be able to finally translate, and play, music that had not been heard for more than three millennia.

He had spent the bulk of the summer in a small triangular room in the attic, annoying the numismatist next door with his constant attempts at articulating the 'music' he was reading.

Today he thought he might finally have it cracked. Abut eleven o'clock in the morning he had finished transcribing the tablets into what he could recognize as music. He started singing.

And hell came to Glasgow University. Witnesses in the corridor said that the walls seemed to shimmer and shake. Some reported an intense, numbing cold, others a stifling heat. But all remembered the deep, atonal chanting that seemed to come from everywhere and nowhere.

The numismatist reports that the wall between the rooms became transparent at one point, and that John Harris himself seemed to be fading in and out of reality.

Out in the museum itself, a party of schoolchildren fled in fright as a stuffed woolly mammoth began to wave its trunk and show suspicious sign of life. Farther back, in the storerooms beyond, a paleontologist was studying a fossil fish when he found he was looking into a deep pool of sea water, with his fossil fish, now suddenly re-animated, swimming happily in it.

Finally, there was a piercing scream. The numismatist had to break open the door, and found Harris on the floor. He was breathing and his eyes were open, but his face was contorted in terror, and his arms were raised as if to ward off an unseen attacker.

The woolly mammoth was found half in and half out of the roped area in which it was displayed. In the storeroom, the paleontologist found that his fossil fish was now embedded in the stone floor beneath his feet.

I raised my head.

"You were here in '87, weren't you?" I asked Doug.

He nodded.

"Do you remember hearing anything about any unbelievable nonsense in the Hunterian Museum?"

He shook his head.

"I'll tell you later. Just keep reading " he said. "It gets better."

It was while Harris was recuperating in hospital that things took a strange turn. Firstly he was visited by two men dressed all in black. They spoke at him rather than with him, and told him that he was messing with forces he couldn't understand. They told him that if he didn't desist, they would be forced to take action. Strangely, after they were gone, nobody in the ward apart from Harris remembered seeing them.

I put the papers down and lit another cigarette.

"What is this shit? It's like a teenager's episode of The Twilight Zone " I said.

"Doo-doo doo-doo " Doug sang, in a passable imitation of the theme tune. "Just keep reading. You must be close to the bit that concerns you by now " he said.

I sighed loudly to let him know how disgusted I was, but in reality I was keen to keep reading. I needed to know how my singing friend was connected to the case...

Harris had another visitor soon afterwards. This man has never been identified, but some have suggested that it was a distant relative of the Johnson who had financed the expedition to Ur. Yet others would have you believe it to be Arthur Dunlop, although why a Glasgow gangster would be interested in esoteric acoustical studies has never been explained. Whoever it was, they were to have a profound effect on John Harris's life afterward.

The man funded Harris's research for the next year. Even while lying in a hospital bed, Harris broke all ties with the scientific establishment, and no more is recorded of his work, either in note form or on any computer we can find.

On leaving hospital, Harris went straight back to the Hunterian Museum. The University wanted to deny him access to any more of their exhibits, but it is recorded that the Museum received a large charitable donation in the winter of '87. After that, Harris had no trouble continuing his studies. It seems his benefactor was at work behind the scenes

Harris immersed himself in the Ur tablets, studying everything that had ever been brought out of the ancient city. Now that he knew how their music was constructed, he was on a quest to translate as much of it as he could find, and find out what uses the people put it to.

It is to be conjectured that the direction of his research was by now being directed by the mysterious benefactor. Whatever the cause, his search took on an increasingly esoteric, even occult, tone. By spring of '88 he had what he believed to be a full incantation, a song used by the peoples of that time to contact their gods.

It is unclear whether Harris actually believed in the power of what he had discovered, or whether it was merely an academic exercise. What is clear is that his benefactor was a believer. An experiment was set up in Maes Howe on Orkney.

It is also clear that the benefactor was a man of some influence, for they were able to hold the test on the spring equinox, inside one of the biggest Neolithic sites in Europe. Apart from Harris, all that is known of the participants is that there were two others, and that one may have been a woman.

Most of what happened next is speculation and is taken from depositions of farmers and other islanders.

At sunset, just as the sun's rays penetrated the inner sanctum of the mound, Harris began his chant. Strange lights were seen in the sky—silver and blue globes of energy that hovered over the Howe and the nearby stone circle, the Ring of Brodgar.

They say that the sound of the singing rang through every stone circle, every burial chamber, in the whole of the northern hemisphere, with reports on file from Malta, Carnac, Germany and from the Serpent Mound in North America. It is even said that vibrations were detected in the stones on Easter Island.

All along the coast of Scotland, Viking longships were seen coming ashore. A busload of Japanese tourists was surprised when a forty-foot serpent dragged itself from Loch Ness and went to sleep on the shore near Urquhart Castle. At Culloden field and Bannockburn the sights and sounds of the old battles were played out, as if time had suddenly gone haywire. At St Andrew's golf course groups of men in plus fours and wielding hickory golf clubs were seen playing the road hole on the 'Old Course'. And in Dunvegan Castle, strange, piping sounds were heard, and the 'Fairy Flag' fluttered in its frame. Out in the North Atlantic, a new volcanic island rose near Surtsey, and a fishing boat went missing just after reporting the appearance of a sea-monster, a kraken nearly a mile long.

Inside the mound on Orkney, reality was becoming fluid.

It is said that the stone walls, Viking graffiti and all, began to fade, and that the people inside were given glimpses of other realities; places where gossamer wings fluttered and thin whistles blew. Great barreled creatures with strange star-shaped extrusions for heads pushed against the thin vein of reality, which started to rip and tear.

Things got very strange after that. Outside the mound, regulars in a bar in Kirkwall told of great moans coming from deep under the sea, as if the ocean floor was splitting. Around the world, the greatest UFO show in history was taking place, with sightings over the White House, the Great Pyramid, Sydney Opera House, and the South Pole Research Station.

Maes Howe was seen to fade in and out of reality. It had almost gone completely when a blue flash lit the night sky over North Scotland. A woman's voice, high-pitched and beautiful, began to sing over the top of Harris.

Harris faltered, and finally stopped. An Orkney farmer would later see two people carrying another away from the Howe. Afterwards, the farmer entered the Howe, and reported seeing strange, five-pointed depressions on the floor, as if the stone itself had melted.

The next day, John Harris was admitted to a private Psychiatric Hospital in the West Coast resort of Ayr. Researchers have been unable to find out who paid his bills. Also on the next day, the Ur tablets were found to be missing from the Hunterian Museum after a visit from two men dressed in black. Maes Howe was closed for 'renovations' after which the five-pointed depressions were no longer visible. The UFO reports were dismissed as sightings of Air Force flares, and the cover- up began.

John Harris remains in the hospital. He apparently still loves music, with a particular penchant for light opera, and Gilbert and Sullivan in particular.

The investigation continues. Were the Men in Black from the Government? Or are our little alien buddies interested in inter-dimensional physics? Why was there so much activity in Montauk on the night the Maes Howe deal went down? Who was the mystery benefactor of John Harris? Did John Harris fall into the clutches of the notorious 'Starry Wisdom' sect? And what actually happened down in the depths of that burial chamber that was grim enough to turn a renowned Doctor of Physics into a physical and emotional wreck.

The truth is waiting to be found.

Postscript:

Since the above was written, in March 1996, John Harris has been released from the hospital. No trace of him has been found, although there have been reported sightings in Orkney, around his old haunts in Glasgow, and on the Giza plateau. Most disturbingly, someone closely fitting his description has recently been photographed near Dulce Air Force base (see http://www.moonlichtnicht.co.uk/ harrisatdulce.jpg), just before a major UFO flap in Phoenix.

The truth is still waiting to be found.

I turned the page and found the referenced photograph. Whoever had been photographed at Dulce, it wasn't John Harris. The guy in the picture was six inches too tall and thirty or forty pounds too heavy.

There were more pictures, and more pages of speculation, but I put them down as Doug looked up from the paper.

"Good stuff, eh?" he said. "The usual mixture of truth, fiction and paranoia."

"So " I said. "How much can I believe?"

"Well " he began, lapsing into his teaching voice, "there was a doctor of physics called John Harris, and he was interested in acoustics, but only on an amateur level—there are no recorded papers in any of the journals. I can't find anything about any shenanigans at the Hunterian or about any untranslated tablets from Ur. And I don't remember any world-wide reports about singing Neolithic sites and massive UFO flaps in spring '88--do you?"

"Maybe the government covered it up?" I said. "Along with Roswell, Area 51, the stargate, HAARP, and Uncle Tom Cobbley and all?"

"You forgot about the Hale-Bopp saucer, the Face on Mars, the Masonic conspiracy in NASA, alien bases underground at Dulce, chemicals in contrails, the third secret of Fatima, the Philadelphia Experiment, Majestic 12 and MK Ultra " Doug said.

"God, they must be busy, these Men in Black " I said. "They've been so successful I've never heard of half of those things."

We both laughed.

I reached over the pile of papers to get another cigarette, and I dislodged the top paper. Underneath there were more pictures, and one of them caught my eye.

The caption read "Mystery man and woman leave the psychiatric hospital in Ayr after visiting John

Harris". I didn't recognize the man, but the woman was unmistakable—it was my client, Mrs. Dunlop.

"So. Does any of it help?" Doug asked.

I sucked my cigarette and flipped through the rest of the photographs. The man— I assumed it was Arthur Dunlop—was in a few more, but she wasn't.

"Oh oh " Doug said, "I know that look. This one's got you going, hasn't it?"

"You don't know the half of it " I said, then I told him about Wee Jimmy, then about my meeting with John Harris. Doug did something I'd never seen him do before. He reached over to the whisky bottle, poured a large measure into the remnants of his coffee, and downed it in one gulp.

He shivered.

"Somebody just walked over my grave " he said. "Do you think it's got something to do with the amulet?"

"I think it's got everything to do with the amulet." I said. "And I'm going to find it, take it to Mrs. Dunlop, and find out just what the fuck is going on."

"Watch your back. I've got a bad feeling about this one " Doug replied.

"I'll be careful."

"That makes me feel soooo much better " he said sarcastically. "Anyway, I can't sit around here all day. I've got the contents of a Bronze Age midden to catalogue."

"Time and shit wait for no man " I said.

That only got a small smile—he really did seem spooked.

"Thanks for the stuff " I said, waving the wad of paper at him as he stood up.

"No problem. I'll run some more searches tonight on John Harris, just to see if there's any more weirdness in your case."

"Please. No more " I said.

He gave me one final wave and left me to the last cup of almost warm coffee.

I read the Harris piece again. It was obvious that Dunlop was the man that paid the hospital bills.

But what did it have to do with me finding the amulet?

I had high strangeness on the Dunlop side of the case and witchcraft on the Durban side. And I also had something inexplicably killing people on the fringes—killing them in the manner of a spook from an eighty-year-old story. This case was, as Doug so succinctly put it, weird shit. I just didn't realize yet how weird it would turn out to be.

Half an hour later I was out on Byres Road. It was raining again, thin, miserable drizzle from a flat, slate-gray sky. I turned up into Hyndland Road just as the rain got heavier.

I had been about to walk—I needed the thinking time. But as the rain got heavier again, I turned right down the lane behind the office and headed for my garage.

The rusting hulk of metal I kept there was almost a motorcar. At one time it had been a perfectly serviceable mode of transport, but the years had not been kind to it. I groaned as I saw how far the rust had spread since my last use of it, some six months before.

The car was small, Japanese, and Shite, with a capital S. But the engine still turned over, the wheels still spun, and no doubt it would get me where I was going. It just wasn't the sort of thing any private eye on five hundred a day should be seen in.

I was on my way to see another name from Wee Jimmy's list: Tommy McIntyre. This one I already knew. Flash Tommy, Pervy Tommy, Uncle Tommy, he had more names than he had brain cells.

He'd arrived in town some five years back. Rumor had it that there were some Brixton Yardies after him—something to do with ten pounds of ganja and a fourteen-year-old girl. He immediately set himself up in the pawnbroking business out in Anniesland, and soon had a growing clientele of woman of a certain age.

Further rumor had it that he did a steady trade in sex toys under the counter—high-class bondage gear for the expensive end of the market. He was also known to fence stolen items— anything from fur coats and tiaras to vintage cars—just as long as it was at the high end of the market. Tommy thought he had a reputation to consider.

Driving to Anniesland was like taking a trip through my past. As I crawled along behind a convoy of buses the high Edwardian buildings loomed over me. There was the pub where I held my twentieth birthday party. There was the flat where I smoked dope for the first and last time, and there was the hotel where Doug got married, and where we got royally plastered on the night his divorce came through.

Along the road a bit was the spot where Andy, a daft flatmate of Doug's, had got beaten up. Well, what did he expect, wearing an SS uniform in Glasgow on a Saturday night? The fact that he'd been going to a fancy dress party had cut no ice with the five or six teenagers who'd played football with him for five minutes before getting bored when he stopped screaming.

Happy days.

I pulled up in front of McIntyres' shop at eleven o'clock. He'd gone up in the world since the last time I was there—there was more gold in his window than I'd seen outside a museum—that is, until I saw Tommy.

You name it, he wore it. Gold chains, three of them around his neck, three huge rings on his right hand, four on his left, including a thumb ring with an opal as big as an eye. He had a stud in each ear and one in his nose.

He saw me looking.

"Would you like to see the one in my belly-button?" he said. "Or the Prince Albert?"

"No, thanks " I said.

"I'm thinking about getting one in my tongue " he said. "The chicks love it." He stuck his tongue out at me and waggled it furiously. I resisted the urge to grab it and tug, hard.

Tommy was stuck in the 70's. He wore a blue polyester suit with a high collar and flared trousers. He had the kind of tan that comes out of an expensive bottle, and his shirt was open nearly to the waist to show it off. He was also just about the hairiest man I'd ever seen. On the top of his head his black, curly mop was beginning to thin and go gray, but his carefully cultivated sideburns were still luxurious, as was the hair on his chest.

He moved aside to let me into the shop, and I saw, slightly disgusted, that he had his nipples pierced with more heavy gold rings. In a younger man it would have been overkill. On Tommy, who was somewhere in his late fifties, it just looked disgusting.

"So what can I do you for, Mr. Adams?" he said.

Our paths had crossed several times. On the first occasion I'd been hired by a wife; to find out whether her husband was playing away. He was, but not with another woman—he had a gay lover, and they bought their play-clothes from Tommy. The second time I'd found a stolen engagement ring—Tommy was selling it for only twice its value.

"I'm looking for an item " I said. "A very peculiar item."

"If it's peculiar you're after, I'm your man " he said. He wasn't wrong there. When he smiled at me I noticed that he'd had his teeth done. His incisors were capped with gold, and a small diamond was fitted in one of his front teeth. It gave him a lop-sided look, and the way it sparkled as he spoke made you look at his mouth rather than his eyes. He probably thought it was sexy.

"So " he said, "How peculiar do you want?"

He reached under the long counter that ran the length of his shop and brought out what looked, at first sight, to be a leather jerkin. He held it up against his body, and I noticed it was indeed leather—a one-piece body suit, with holes cut for nipples and genitals. He poked his finger through the bottom hole and wiggled it around.

"Interested?" he said.

"Not even remotely " I responded.

"I've got it in rubber as well?" he said. "Red or black."

I shook my head.

"Save it for your perverts " I said.

He looked shocked.

"A love of experimentation is not perversion. Don't you ever play games?"

"Oh, aye. But I've got something your customers seem to lack. An imagination."

"If you've come here to insult me " he said.

I shook my head, suddenly weary—weary of talking to sleazy people in sleazy places, weary of pounding the streets for little reward.

"I'm after the Johnson Amulet " I said.

His eyes went wide.

"What. No wandering around the subject? No verbal fencing to see if I know anything? You're losing your touch, Mr. Adams." He chuckled. I could see that he felt he was ahead of the game on this one. I lobbed him another easy one to see if he would take.

"I'm working for Artie Dunlop " I said.

He didn't flicker.

"I know " he said. "A wee birdie told me."

This was getting me nowhere. Short of physical intimidation—and believe me, I was tempted—I would have to wait and see what he could tell me, if anything. I was building myself up to threaten him when the door behind me opened. I turned, and nearly got a faceful of breasts.

She was statuesque; I'll give her that much. She wore red plastic, thigh-length leather boots, with an eight-inch stiletto. Above that, a black leather mini-skirt that barely protected her modesty, a black leather halter top that just covered her nipples, and nothing else. With the added height of the boots she must have been six-four or six-five.

She wore a long blonde wig that reached almost to her waist. She'd had a boob job, a lip job, a nose job, an eye job and a face-lift—and that was just the bits I could see. She wanted to be Pamela Anderson, but she was never going to make it. The body was nearly there, but the face was wound up so tight it looked like it might split at any minute.

"Mr. Adams " Tommy said. "Meet Mandy. She looks after my specialist ladies line."

"Pleasedtameetcha " she said through her gum. She was trying for Hollywood, but the wee girl from Paisley showed through.

She walked past me, and Tommy gave her bum a squeeze as it was on the way past.

"Like two oranges in a bag " he said, and let out his best lecherous laugh. Mandy never looked back, just sashayed through to the office at the rear. She nearly carried it off, but the effect was spoiled when she went over on her ankle and swore, a loud, definitely Scottish, "Ya fucking bastard".

"Mandy and I have got an 'arrangement', if you know what I mean?" Tommy said, and dropped a long slow wink.

"What, she cooks and you wash up?" I said. I stopped him before he could reply—the details of Tommy MacIntyre's love life were not something I wanted to hear.

"Why don't you just tell me about the amulet?" I asked.

Tommy was enjoying himself.

"You want to know if anybody's tried to fence the ugly thing?" he said to me. "You want to know if I know who's got it, or who wants it?"

"Yep " I said, grinding my teeth. "I've got a fifty waiting nice and warm in my wallet for the right gen."

"Make it a ton, and come back at eight tonight " he said. "I'll have something for you."

I looked him in the eye, but all I saw was the usual animal cunning. Tommy survived on feel and instinct. He reminded me of a hyena.

I left him my card, one of the legit ones. It still said "Adams Detection Corporation" but the phone number was right.

"You'd better not be dicking me around " I said.

"Mr. Adams " he said, full of mock shock, "as if I would, when I've got all my other wonderful customers 'dicking' around all the time."

I left him playing with the leather one-piece and went back out into the clean air outside.

I felt like I needed a wash. Visiting Tommy was like visiting a porn shop and, as a little old lady passed me, I lowered my eyes, suddenly guilty.

That was it. I was out of ideas. Short of visiting every pawnbroker in town—all of whom wouldn't touch an Artie Dunlop piece with a bargepole—I only had Durban, Tommy McIntyre, and Dunlop himself. I resolved to visit Durban again, rattle his cage and see if any feathers flew.

I got back in the car and headed back to the office

The journey back took nearly an hour. The rain was back, heavier than ever. And some dickhead of a delivery driver thought it would be a great idea to double park in Hyndland Road at noon. Mothers were trying to get kids from school, business people were trying to get to lunch, and I quietly poisoned myself by chain-smoking Camels in a closed box of Japanese tin. I wasn't in the best of humor by the time I got the car back to the garage.

I thought about going up to the office, but all that was there was a half-empty bottle of whisky and a book I didn't want to read. Instead, I went to the bank and withdrew a hundred pounds. The assistant didn't smile at me this time.

I took the underground down to the city center—the car would have been worse than useless in the rain and the traffic. Anyway, I knew I would have a drink at some point in the afternoon. It was just a matter of how long I could fight off the urge.

It turned out not to be long at all. Wednesday was early closing. It was after one o'clock when I got off the tube. The lights were off in Durban and Lamberts by the time I got there. There was no sign of movement in the shop, no silver Rover outside. I couldn't even slow myself down with a coffee—the cafe was also closed down for the day. I resigned myself to the inevitable, and headed for The Blythswood Bar.

Glasgow had changed a lot over my drinking years. Banks had become bars, bars had become building societies, and building societies had become trendy café-bars where booze is double the price and conversation half as intelligent. The Blythswood was one of my anchors against progress.

I'm sure the place has changed over the years, but if so, the changes have been gradual—a new carpet here, a replaced light fitting there. This wasn't a trendy bar. It didn't have a theme, it didn't allow youngsters to hang around the bar drinking bottled mixtures of spirit and soft drinks, and it didn't have any no-smoking or kids-allowed seating areas. This was a bar where men drank whisky, chased it down with beer, and talked about football, horses, politics and religion. I liked it—buying a beer in here felt like snuggling down in a favorite armchair.

The barman handed me the beer after wiping the excess foam from the sides of the glass.

"I see the Gers have signed another Dutchman " he said. I grunted at him. That was usually enough to show that I wasn't interested in talking about football.

"Fucking Orange bastards " a voice said to my left. Actually, what he said was "Fukin owange batarts", but if I'm going to tell this, I'm going to have to tone down the accents. This was a real Glasgow bar, with real Glasgwegian's talking. It's sometimes incomprehensible, even to those of us who live here. Imagine Billy Connelly, in a manic mood, after more than a few beers, and you're not even getting close.

"Fenian wanker " another voice said to my right.

"Language " the barman said.

"Naw, it isnae, it's abuse " the man on the left said. "But never mind, you're no fae Glesca, so ye cannae be expected to know the difference."

At that the man on my left bought the man on my right a drink, and they started talking about the forthcoming 4:30 race at Kempton Park. I moved away and tuned them out.

On another day, in another part of town, that conversation might have led to more serious abuse then shouting, followed by punching, kicking, biting and, occasionally, the use of a knife. But one of the reasons I liked this pub in particular was that it was one of the places where sectarianism and tribal loyalties were forgotten—the booze was the important thing here. I took my beer over to a table in the corner, cleared my head, and watched the world go by.

This too was part of the case. When a case started to work on me, started to take over all my waking thoughts, I always let it go for a while. And for me, the only way to do that was to get into town and lose myself among people.

It was a habit I'd picked up years ago, even before I got into this business. After Liz, I was at a loss for a long time. I drifted from one part-time job to another, and served beer in too many bars on too many Saturday nights. It was Doug who suggested the journalism correspondence course, and picked up the tab for the fee.

For two years I'd written, swotted, and written some more. I passed the course exam at the end, and got a job on a small provincial newspaper.

It was soul destroying. I was no better than a dogsbody—making coffee, running errands, and only on very few occasions getting to cover a local event. The highlight of my year was the local flower show, where I got to write a ten-line filler on a vegetable shaped like a penis.

That was when I started drinking to escape. I'd almost escaped completely at several times over the years, but Doug had always dragged me back from the brink.

The crisis came on the fifth anniversary of Liz's death. I'd arranged to meet Doug at seven in the evening for a few beers and a curry, but by the time he turned up I was already well to my way to oblivion. He took me home, sobered me up, and told me I'd be dead in a year if I didn't slow down.

"Good " I said, but even then, in my blackest depression, I knew I didn't mean it. Suicide had been big in my mind in the first week after I'd found Liz, but I hadn't done it then, and I knew I never would. Not the quick way, anyway.

"You need to do something, man " Doug had said. "What do you want to do with your life?"

"Fight bad guys, save the world, get the girl, all that happy shit. I want to be Arnold- fucking-Schwarzenneger " I growled at him.

"No can do " said Doug. "Your head's not big enough. But if that's what you want, why not join the cops?" I shook my head. "Or become a private dick?" he said, and it was as if a light bulb came on over my head—a big one with the word 'IDEA' written on it.

And I had done it. Doug had thought I was joking, but three months later I left the paper and set myself up in the office in Byres Road. My first client was a wee man called Pete Mulville, who had lost his wife. He hadn't lost her, she'd run off with an aerobics instructor from Kelvinside called Marco, but he still paid me, and I was off and running.

Mostly I enjoyed the work. I met a lot of people, my time was mainly my own, and I didn't have anybody to report to other than my clients. But sometimes the cases got too much and, like today, I hit the bars.

I came out of my reverie, brought back to the present by a commotion at a table near the bar. A large woman, eyes red and mascara running down her cheeks, had just slapped her companion, a small weasel-like man with thinning hair and the biggest overbite I'd ever seen.

"You're no gentleman " she shouted at him.

By now the whole bar was watching the little man with interest. My money was on him slapping her back, harder—there was something in his eyes that said he'd done it before.

"And you're no lady " he said to her. The bar was so quiet that even though he had spoken softly, everybody heard.

"Get yourself cleaned up " he said, even softer. "I won't have you making a fool of me in public."

The woman stood. We all saw that she was at least three times his size as she teetered to the washroom on heels that were made for a much thinner woman.

It was only after she was out of earshot that the little man turned to the rest of us.

"She isnae mine " he said. "I'm breaking her in for a friend."

Half the people in the bar laughed, the tension broke, and we all went back to ignoring each other. When the woman returned her mascara was gone and she sat down meekly opposite the man. They spoke in silence for a while before leaving. He led, she followed.

They'd left me thinking about partners. Partners and friends, Liz and Jimmy. It was time to move on.

The rain had eased slightly. I strolled down to Charing Cross, mentally noting the new buildings, the shiny glass corporate offices that were slowly replacing the old weary Victorian stone.

As I crossed the M8 motorway the rain started to fall heavily again, and gave me just the excuse I needed to pop into the Bon Accord. I stayed there for hours, drinking heavy, strong Scottish ales with names like Skullsplitter and Bitter And Twisted. I talked to nobody, and nobody talked to me. By the time six o'clock came around my legs were a bit less secure than usual, and my head was nicely fuzzy.

A long walk in the rain through Kelvingrove Park and along University Avenue sobered me up a bit, but not enough to let me drive back to Anniesland. I ate fish and chips standing outside my favorite chippie in Byres Road before hailing a taxi to take me to Tommy MacIntyre's shop.

"Tommy McIntyre, eh?" the cab driver said, and leered at me in his rear-view mirror. "Are you going for anything special?"

"Aye " I said. "A diamante stud for the end of my knob, and a titanium column to go through my scrotum."

"Oh, aye " he said, and his gaze slid away from the mirror. "Very nice."

He didn't speak to me for the rest of the journey, which was fine by me. He dropped me off in front of MacIntyre's shop at five-to-eight. He took my fare, didn't even quibble about a tip, and was off and away almost before I'd shut the cab door.

The shop sat in darkness. That in itself wasn't unusual—it was past dark, on a weekday, and trade would be light, at best. I peered through the main window. The light was on in the office at the back, and I saw movement, as if someone had walked in front of a lamp.

I knocked on the window—I'd been about to shout when I realized how futile it would be; I wasn't operating at top speed. I went round to the door, to knock louder, and was surprised to find the door ajar. I pushed it open and stepped inside.

The streetlights didn't penetrate this far, and I found myself stumbling in semi-darkness. I hit something, a piece of furniture. A loud crash echoed in the room. At the far end I caught a glimpse of movement again, a swift shadow that was quickly gone.

I called out.

"Hey, Tommy. I've got that money I promised you." I realized as I spoke that I had spent a large part of it that afternoon. But Tommy wasn't to know that yet.

I moved further up the room. My eyes started to adjust to the gloom, and I saw that the door to the office was slightly open.

"I hope you're not giving Mandy one in there " I shouted. "That's a sight I definitely don't want to see."

And that's when my brain caught up with what my nose had been telling it for the last ten seconds. The place stank—the same rancid odor I'd smelled in my flat two nights ago. Suddenly my legs went weak and threatened to give under me. I forced myself forward until my hand was on the door to the office.

"Are you there, Tommy?" I said, and noticed with dismay how throaty and scared I sounded. I gathered up what courage I could and pushed the office door open.

Thirty seconds later I was back out in the road, gasping for air and trying to keep down a suddenly acidic combination of beer and fried food.

Tommy McIntyre wasn't going to be giving Mandy anything. He lay in a pathetic heap on the floor of his office, a sad, middle-aged man wearing a one-piece leather jump suit. There were more holes in it now—red, suppurating holes that still oozed blood. And there were holes, each about an inch diameter, in his cheek, in his thighs, and in his neck. A pool of blood spread beneath him.

But worst of all, and the thing that had sent me running for air, was the larger hole, the one where his genitals had been, now just an open, weeping sore.

I finally got myself under control. I turned and walked quickly away, turning off the main road as soon as I could and working my way through the warren of streets until I was far enough away to feel safe hailing a cab. I had him take me to The Rock at the top end of Hyndland Road. Hardy and Newman would be looking for me, and I didn't want to make it too hard on them— I knew the conversation with them had been coming all day—Tommy's death just brought it closer.

I knew my prints were all over Tommy's shop. I could have gone back in, tried to wipe them clean, but I had been blundering around all over the place. Besides, I didn't particularly want to come face to face with whatever had attacked Tommy.

I also remembered giving him my card. And Mandy would remember me. She hadn't looked that bright, but her memory had to be good for at least a couple of hours. I got to The Rock and ordered a whisky. Suddenly I felt sober, and I determined to rectify that situation as soon as possible.

I'd chosen The Rock for a reason. Newman and Hardy knew it was my local. I'd been going in there for more than twenty years now. I was in there the night the Falkland War broke out and four of the locals signed up for the army. I was there the night the one-armed man won the eight- ball pool competition, and I was there the night they started tearing the old pub down to 'modernize' the interior. I hadn't been back as often since then—it sold food now, and let kids in—but it was still one of the places I always ended up when someone needed to find me.

I was near the end of my fourth or fifth whisky when I felt the hand of the law on my shoulder.

"Mr. Adams " Hardy said. "We'd like to ask you a few questions."

"Ask away " I said.

The man next to me made a mistake.

"Leave the man alone, why can't you? He's just having a drink " he said, then backed away fast as Newman appeared at his side.

"Do you have a problem wi' cops, wee man?" the policeman said.

"No. No… I didnae ken ye were the police….I...."

Newman left him alone and turned his attentions on me.

"Down the station, please " he said.

I drained my whisky in one—it looked like it would my last one for a while—and went with them.

We got out into the fresh air, and my legs started to buckle. The day finally caught up with me.

Hardy grabbed me by the arm and hauled me upwards, but the movement was too fast. I gagged, and out it came—a partially digested fish supper, a couple of pints of beer, and four whiskies. Most of it went over my own trousers, but some caught Newman, almost covering the left foot of his black, shiny, shoes—only they weren't shiny any more.

"You dirty wee bastard " one of them said. By that stage I wasn't sure who. I saw the fist coming, but wasn't able to roll away from it. It knocked me to the ground, and the last thing I saw before everything went black was the toe of a shoe heading for my head.

I woke up in the drunk cell at Maryhill Police Station. It hadn't changed much since my last visit some twelve years before—it still stank of piss and vomit, and the graffiti was still graphic, if crudely done. My head felt like someone had stepped on it, and when I touched it just above my ear I felt the lump of a developing bruise.

I had been stripped to my underpants, and given a coarse sheet to wrap around myself. My clothes were not in the cell. My cigarettes were at the foot of the bench I'd been lying on, with a box of safety matches—I obviously wasn't to be trusted with the Zippo.

My hands shook as I lit a cigarette, and not just from the cold. I was about as miserable as I could get, and it wasn't over yet; I still had 'Stan and Ollie' to face.

They made me wait, though. I had smoked five cigarettes before someone came for me. A young policeman that I didn't know led me to Interview Room One.

It had changed. They'd installed a wall-mounted tape recorder since my last visit, but I doubted if Newman and Hardy ever switched it on. They were waiting, the two of them on the same side of the desk. I sat down opposite them and lit up another Camel.

"Do I get a phone call?" I asked.

"Later " Hardy said.

"In the morning " Newman said.

"And are you holding me on anything?"

"Drunk and disorderly " Hardy said, smiling.

"And resisting arrest " Newman added.

"Do you guys have to do that?" I asked.

"Do..." said Hardy.

"...what?" said Newman, and they both smiled at me. It was like being smiled at by a pair of hungry tigers.

"Tell us about McIntyre " Hardy said.

"Tommy McIntyre? I was round at his shop earlier " I said. "I'm looking for something and I thought he might be able to help me find it."

I expected them to ask what it was that I was looking for, but either they already knew or they were saving it for later.

"John Harris, Jimmy Allen, and now Tommy McIntyre " Newman said. "All dead, all with the same M.O. and all not long after talking to you. Are you beginning to see a pattern here?"

"Tommy's dead? When? I only saw him this..."

I didn't get a chance to finish.

"Tommy's hoor Mandy eyeballed you this afternoon, and we've got the cab driver who took you to The Rock at ten past eight. Your wee business card was in Tommy's jacket pocket, with the time—'eight o'clock' written on the back. Do you want to bet your prints are in the shop?" Hardy said.

"And we've got a wifie who says she saw you on the bus yesterday with John Harris. She said you were acting pally with him " Newman said.

I shivered.

"Can I at least get my clothes back?"

"Forensics " Newman said.

"Might take a while " Hardy said.

"Now about Pervy Tommy?" Newman said.

I told them my story, from start to finish. The only thing I left out was who I was working for, and what I was looking for.

"That trip to Dunblane?" Hardy said.

"Awfully convenient for you " Newman said.

"Aye " I said. "I suppose it's the only reason I'm not sitting here charged with murder?"

"There's time yet " Newman said.

"Plenty of time " said Hardy.

It was all downhill from there. They went over my story time and time again, looking for cracks, hoping for an inconsistency. I chain-smoked Camels, and they got more agitated. There was a window high on the wall above me and thin watery sunlight was beginning to seep in when they finally stopped.

Newman left the room, while Hardy just sat and stared at me. Newman came back with a pile of clothes and dropped them on the table in front of me. The stink of stale vomit assaulted my nasal passages.

"No blood. No bits of Tommy McIntyre " he said. "And the coroner is now saying that the wounds were caused by an animal—some kind of exotic snake he's never seen before."

"That doesn't mean you're off the hook " Hardy said.

"Aye. We'll be keeping an eye on you " Newman said.

"I know " I said. "Don't leave town, stay in touch, all that happy-crappy."

"Aye. You know the drill " Hardy said.

"Just hope that nobody else you talk to turns up dead " Newman said.

"You mean like the pair of you?" I said, and smiled as I saw a momentary shock in both their eyes. I had finally got to 'Stan and Ollie'.

That thought kept me mildly happy as I dressed then signed at the desk for my watch, keys, wallet and lighter. I felt sure I should have had more money in the wallet, but I wasn't in a position to argue.

The sun was just coming up as I left the station and headed down the steps to Maryhill Road. An office cleaner passed me, and she looked me up and down before turning up her nose.

"Rough night, son?" she said.

I grunted at her, and lit another cigarette. Combined with my first fresh air for twelve hours, it brought on a fit of coughing.

She stepped back away from me.

"If you're going to throw up, do it over in the bushes " she said, pointing me over to her left. "It's my turn to do the steps, and I don't need any more shit than I get already."

I nodded—I wasn't ready to speak again just yet.

The rain had finally stopped, and the streets glistened silver in the new sun. Milkmen and paperboys were out and about, and young executives keen to make their mark revved up their BMWs.

The town was waking up for the day, but it was welcome to it. I trudged wearily home, dropped my clothes on the bedroom floor, and fell into bed. I was unconscious in seconds.

Four

I didn't wake up again till gone one o'clock in the afternoon. I stood under the coldest shower for ten minutes, and even then it took two coffees and a cigarette to get my brain into gear. There was a pervading stink of stale vomit in the bedroom, and it was only then that I remembered the sickness on my trousers. After consigning all of yesterday's clothes to the washing machine I went to search my admittedly sparse wardrobe.

I had to settle for a very old pair of black jeans that were faded to a charcoal gray, and a white cotton shirt that had been pulled and twisted until it looked like I carried several bags of potatoes under it. I partially covered it with a black waistcoat, but I looked too much like an extra from The Godfather that it had to go. I found an old black cord jacket that looked slightly better. All I needed was Doug's spectacles and I'd look like a schoolteacher. And least I didn't look like I meant to kill anybody.

I realized that I felt ready for work, raring to go. Sometime during the night, or maybe during my sleep,

I'd finished mourning Wee Jimmy, and my maudlin period over Liz had passed for a couple more months.

I poured another coffee. It had stewed to a thick black consistency that was just about what I needed at that point.

I was ready. I sat at my desk and lifted The Little Sister from the drawer. Five minutes later I was lost completely, and it was only when I lifted my coffee and found it was cold that I came back. I'd been away, to somewhere where men were men and lost woman with problems were not all that they seemed. I knew what he meant.

I noticed with a shock that it was getting on for three o'clock. Tonight was the night that Durban went out to play with his 'old folk', and I meant to find out what went on—I'd have to get a move on if I wanted to be in place at the right time to follow him.

I checked the weather before going out, and realized that I'd need a coat. I chose my long cream Macintosh. I belted it up, turned up the collar, and did my Bogey impressions in front of the mirror for a while. I still couldn't keep a cigarette in my mouth for more than five seconds at a time—I'd never fathom how he did it. I decided against the trilby. I'd bought it a long time ago, but never had the nerve to wear it out in Glasgow. There's only so much abuse that I was prepared to take.

There was no mail in the box at the bottom of the stairs, not even any bills, which was just as well—I was spending my fee just about as fast as I was making it. In that last hour before Newman and Hardy turned up in The Rock, I'd bought too many drinks for people I didn't know, and they were only too happy to take them. Then again, I'd just made a couple of hundred pounds while locked up in a police station. That story might get me some of the drinks back the next time I was in.

I had a long look around the parked cars when I got to street level, but there were no police-types loitering in the area. Either Stan and Ollie weren't having me followed yet, or policemen had got a lot better at blending in with their environment.

Although it was raining, the sun, low in the sky and slanting through thin cloud, hurt my eyes, and I was seriously thinking about investing in a pair of sunglasses. Then I remembered that I lived in Glasgow—it wasn't worth it, not for ten days out of a year.

Old Joe was in his usual place behind the counter in the newsagents. He saw me coming and waved two packs of cigarettes at me—Camels in one hand, Marlboro in the other. He raised an eyebrow. I plumped for the Marlboro; my throat wouldn't take much more of the others.

He also handed me an early edition of the Evening Express.

"I missed you this morning, Derek. Out working?"

"Aye. Something like that " I said, but didn't elaborate. Joe had one of the loosest mouths in town, and it wouldn't be good business if it got around that I'd spent a night with Glasgow's finest boys in blue.

Not that the news wouldn't get around quickly enough anyway—the bush telegraph was highly efficient in this part of Glasgow. I just didn't see why I should be the one to set it going.

Joe seemed distracted, though. He had begun talking again almost before I'd answered him.

"It's a shame about auld Jimmy. Who would dae a thing like that to an old man? Hanging's too good for the likes of them."

I muttered something that I hoped sounded like agreement, not wanting to get drawn into the argument. Joe believed that all of society's ills would be cured by bringing back the birch, locking up everyone under the age of twenty-one, then putting them in the army. He also advocated the automatic death penalty for anything involving bodily harm, forced repatriation for all non-whites, and the cutting off of body parts for theft.

Some days I knew how he felt and even came close to agreeing with him, but today wasn't one of them.

"Anyway " he said, "the funeral's tomorrow—twelve o'clock at St Bridget's in Clarkston. Will I see you there?"

"Aye, sure " I said. "I'll come and see the old chap off. Somebody's got to."

"Oh, you needn't worry on that score. The old man had plenty of friends. There'll be a big turnout."

I gave him a wave as I left. He went back to standing still behind the counter. The old man stood there, day in, day out, for more than fifteen hours. He had a wife who took over to allow him time to eat, but the rest of the time he stood there, from six a.m. to nine p.m. every day including Christmas. It was either dedication or stupidity. I wasn't sure which, but I wished I had his stamina.

I also wished he'd find something new to sing—it had been 'Just One Cornetto' for ten years now, and at times I could cheerfully strangle him. Today, though, I gave him a smile as I left. I didn't tell him that three of the people I'd talked to in the last forty-eight hours were dead. He'd probably stay behind the counter and wait for it to come for him.

It was only when I got to the car and threw the paper down on the passenger seat that I noticed the headline:

UNCLE KILLER STRIKES AGAIN
Pawnbrokers close all over the city as terror strikes

Beneath that there was an old picture of Tommy McIntyre and some sparse details of his murder. From the story it was obvious that the police weren't giving out any info. I guessed that some of the more prurient information came from Mandy. Sure enough, on page three there was a full- length picture of her in a bikini. I nearly choked when I read the text.

Mandy McDowell, 29, a glamour model, was the last person to see the deceased alive. She had entered his shop in search of some fashionable lingerie to wear at a photo shoot later in the day. McIntyre, 58 , known in the trade as Pervy Tommy, had obviously been attracted to her charms and made a crude pass at her. She left the shop, disgusted. That was at seven o'clock yesterday evening, barely an hour before the police found his mutilated body in the back office. "He was an old pervert " Miss McDowell sobbed. "But nobody deserves to die like that."

'Glamour model'? '29'? The reporter obviously hadn't looked too closely. On second thought, maybe he had—the picture that accompanied the piece had obviously been airbrushed. Some smarter reporter had linked Tommy's death to auld Jimmy's, but that was all they were able to do. 'Stan and Ollie' wouldn't give them any more unless they thought it would advance the case. I knew that from long experience

I checked the full article three times, but my name wasn't mentioned, not even as someone helping the police with their inquiries. I said a prayer of thanks for small mercies as I drove away

Twenty minutes later I was back in the coffee shop opposite Durban and Lambert's premises, nursing another cup of strong coffee and trying not to wallow too deeply in self-pity. It wasn't working too well—a night in the cells has that kind of effect on a body

It wasn't as if it was the first time I had been pulled in. The first had been while I was still a first year student

We had been out on the town—the happy wanderers, Doug, three others, and myself hitting all the bars in Byres Road. Doug and I had come out of the Aragon, having failed as usual to pull any nurses, when three policemen approached us. Two took me to one side while the third led Doug and the others off. Ten minutes later I found myself in Patrick police station, being grilled on suspicion of rape

I knew I was innocent, but they didn't. It was 'Where were you on Tuesday 20th, November' and 'Did you know Caroline Moore' and 'Where did you get rid of the knife you used to threaten her'. After a night of none-too-friendly questioning, they let me go. When they finally caught the right man his picture was plastered all over the front of the evening paper. For me, it was like looking into a mirror

That had been the first time. Others had followed, several times for being found in the street too drunk to move, once for doing a favor for Wee Jimmy that turned into somebody trying to kill me, and me having to put somebody in hospital to save myself

More recently I'd been brought in under the kindly eyes of Newman and Hardy on one pretence or another, and for various degrees of seriousness. Nothing before had ever been as bad as last night, though

The waitress asking me if I wanted 'some fancies' jerked me awake. I hadn't noticed that I was in danger of falling asleep over my coffee. I fought off the urge for facetiousness and politely refused. Maybe I was getting more mature. On the other hand, maybe I was just tired

Eileen wasn't on duty—I didn't know whether to be happy or sad at the fact

"Is Eileen around?" I asked the waitress, who had just moved along to the next table

"No, sir " she said. She was polite, but her eyes told a different story. "She's got the day off. But Mr. Durban's still in the shop.", ,

So Eileen had told the other waitresses? That didn't bother me—if anything happened in the antique shop from now on, I was sure to get to know about it, now that they knew there was a tenner available for the right information

There wasn't much activity around Durban and Lambert's, and I found my mind wandering, trying to make connections, but I still couldn't figure out who had killed the three men, or what it had to do with the amulet. I suspected that Dunlop was at the center of it all. I'd have to get round to interviewing him, and sooner rather than later. Thinking of him reminded me that I hadn't talked to my client for more than thirty-six hours

This time her phone rang three times before she replied

"Mr. Adams " she said, before I even spoke. "Are you any closer to finding it?", ,

"Every day in every way I'm getting closer and closer " I said. I didn't get any laughs this time

"My husband is most anxious that you retrieve it " she said. "He is getting ill with worry.", ,

"You could try singing to him?" I said. "A bit of light opera? 'Three Little Maids from School' maybe?", ,

I heard the sharp intake of breath on the other end of the line

"You have been a busy boy " she said. "But don't get distracted with peripherals. The amulet is the thing you're getting paid to investigate, not my private life."

I wasn't too sure that they weren't inherently intertwined, but I let it ride for now

"I need to talk to your husband " I said

Her voice rose, and I heard anger in it

"No " she almost shouted. "Find the amulet. And find it fast.", ,

"But...", ,

"No. Don't you understand? If you don't find it soon, maybe even tonight, then more will die. Many more."

A cold chill settled in my spine

"If I find out you were responsible for any of those deaths I'll make sure you rot in hell " I said

She gave a hollow laugh

"I probably will anyway Mr. Adams…I probably will anyway." Then she hung up on me again. I rang Doug.

"Hey Derek." he said. "I came round to The Rock last night and Tom at the bar said that the boys in blue had you. And I heard about Tommy McIntyre. Is everything okay?"

"Hunky dory " I said. "I'm now a major suspect in three murders my client is pissed off with me and I spewed up all over Stan Newman's shoes. Things couldn't be better."

"Well hold on to your hat " Doug said. "Here comes a newsflash. It's just been on the television that police want to interview an old Arabian gentleman who has been seen in the vicinity of two of the murders."

"They never told me about that " I said.

"They were probably waiting for you to mention it " Doug said.

"Aye. That's their style."

I thought for a bit.

"Did you find out anything more on Dunlop or the Amulet?" I asked.

"Just one thing " Doug said. "But you'll like it. Artie Dunlop is the great-grandson of the Dunlop who wrote the book the archaeologist at the dig in Ur."

I thanked him promised him a couple of free beers and went back to my coffee.

I knew already that the name must be significant… now I had it confirmed. Things were beginning to fall into place and I now had a theory concerning a feud over the artifacts brought back from the dig. All I had to do was find out who the feuding parties were and I'd finally have a cast-iron suspect. At the moment all I had was Durban.

After an hour I noticed that two people had gone in to the antique shop and not come back out.

The first was a grandiose lady in high heels fur coat and hat looking like a refugee from one of those BBC character dramas set in an old country house. I was willing to bet that her handbag contained an expensive compact and perfumed handkerchief alongside some of those exclusive Russian cigarettes with the gold band around the filter.

She walked with the air of command head held high the sun glinting off her pearls and drop earrings. If she was a day under seventy I would be very much surprised.

The second was a very old gentleman in a tweed suit with a battered trilby and a tartan bow tie. He needed help getting out of the taxi that brought him and he only made it across the curb by leaning heavily on an ancient oak walking stick.

He looked like he had come down in the world—his suit showed signs of wear and his shoes were scuffed badly at the toes but he still had the bearing and gait of an old military man. He also had the finest moustache I'd ever seen stretching out three inches on either side of his cheeks and waxed to stiff points. He resembled nothing more than an old lion thrown out of the pride wounded and running out of time fast.

Durban actually came out of the shop and helped him up the steps; otherwise the old man would have been trying for the rest of the afternoon.

There were several other customers but these all left at some point. None of them looked in the least furtive and several carried expensively wrapped packages under their arms.

At four o'clock the closed sign went up. I paid my bill and went to sit in the car trying to look inconspicuous. Luckily I didn't have long to wait—there was an over-officious traffic warden nearby who knew I only had a couple of minutes left on the meter I'd parked beside.

Five minutes later Durban left with the two I had seen earlier and got into a car parked just down the street. I had a momentary panic when my car's engine turned over but wouldn't kick into life.

"Come on darling—be nice " I whispered and she responded not quite purring like a cat more croaking like a toad as I got going and followed at a discreet distance.

It wasn't easy—Durban was a very careful very slow driver and I found myself almost screaming in frustration as we crawled through the city headed south. I managed to drop into place three cars behind them as we wandered slowly through the early rush hour traffic going across the Kingston Bridge. I needn't have bothered; Durban was very much an 'eyes forward at all times' driver.

As usual the dual carriageway had attracted its fair share of dick-heads and I was cut off on several occasions but I always managed to keep Durban in sight. I had a bad moment when I thought they were headed for the airport but they kept on going past the turn-off then headed down the slip road for Irvine and North Ayrshire. Traffic was thinner now and I had to hang further back.

Luckily the car was quite distinctive—there weren't any other old 1960's Rovers on the road and I had little trouble following as they headed out into the country

I had stopped concentrating, singing along to an old Elvis number on the radio, so I nearly missed it when they pulled off into a roadside petrol station in Beith. I just managed to get in to the forecourt behind them, taking a small delight in making the jerk behind me brake hard—he'd been driving just three feet from me, trying to get me to go faster. He obviously wasn't paying attention or he'd have known that my tin bucket was going at top speed anyway

There was a problem with pulling in to the station though—I found myself only three feet away from the Rover's back bumper at the petrol pumps

What followed was pure pantomime. I got out of my car turned half backwards, having to twist my whole body round so that Durban couldn't see my face. He was already out of the Rover and walking around it to the pumps. He passed within two yards of me but didn't raise his head

I got round the back of my car and got fuel in, all the time with my back to the car in front

"Hey, Jimmy " a voice said, and I turned to see a pimply youth at the parallel pump. "They don't have CCTV—if you're going to run without paying, just do it. The cops round here are too lazy to chase you."

I tried to look shocked

"I'm not going without paying " I said

"Oh, yeah " the kid said in an American accent. "Tell it to the judge."

Sometimes it gets like that—everybody you meet is trying to be someone else

By this time Durban was already on his way to the kiosk to pay. I finished up quickly and followed behind, all the time trying to keep my face hidden

I dropped into the queue two places behind him. He walked right past me after he'd paid, but I pretended to look at the newspapers and he didn't glance my way

They had fresh doughnuts at the counter—thick, floury things coated in sugar. Usually they wouldn't have appealed at all, but my stomach suddenly reminded me that I hadn't eaten all day. I bought a bag of six

Once I'd paid I was too busy congratulating myself on my skill at avoiding Durban and turned away from the counter, right into the face of the old lady in the fur coat

She squealed, a small, almost dog-like bark of surprise, and dropped her purse, scattering small coins all over the floor where they proceeded to run under the counters as if they'd been pulled there on strings

I scrabbled around with her on the floor, both of us apologizing all the time. I kept one eye on the door, expecting at any moment to see Durban come to check on the woman

"You're so kind " she said to me as I finally helped her upright, wincing as the old bones in her knees cracked loudly. Now that I saw her up close I had to revise her age upwards. Wrinkles hung slackly at her neck, and her hands were covered with liver spots. I was glad I hadn't given her a bigger shock; she didn't look like she would have survived it

She looked me up and down

"You know " she whispered, her voice conspiratorial, "it's so good to see a young man dressed properly. But you need a tie, dear. A nice sensible tie. Maybe I could take you shopping?"

I couldn't believe it—she was flirting with me. I muttered something non-committal and left before I burst into hysterical laughter. I managed to get to the car without Durban looking my way and I pretended to root around in the doughnut bag until the woman finally came out of the shop.

My heartbeat was up, my palms were sweaty, but I was enjoying myself, more than I had for a long time. I almost, but not quite, fought off an attack of the giggles.

The smell from the doughnut bag was cloying and sickly. I scrunched it up, doughnuts and all, and threw it in the back seat, where it joined the old newspapers, empty cigarette packets and soft-drink cans. In centuries to come someone like Doug would have a field day describing 'A Twentieth Century midden'.

When Durban got going I let them have a five second start before following on behind. Somewhere between Dalry and Kilwinning—I'm a bit vague on anywhere outside the city—they pulled into the drive of a large Victorian house sitting on its own in several hundred acres of land. The old Rover swished through the gates and, five seconds later, just as I got to them, the gates swung shut. Even from inside the car I could hear the satisfying clunk as they locked into place.

I drove past, only having time to notice that there were at least six cars in the driveway. A hundred yards down the road things opened out to open field once more. I did a tight three-point- turn in the road, went back, and looked for somewhere to park.

It took a few minutes, but I found the perfect spot: a mud track off the main road that ran into a disused yard adjoining one of the house's walls. I turned off the engine and rolled down the windows but there was no noise, just the warbling of birds and the soft rustling of the wind in the trees. I was instantly reminded of childhood conker hunting through sepulchral woodland. There is an oppressive feel to woodland that I've never gotten to grips with—concrete and street lamps were more my scene.

The wall was over six feet high, and I had to do a bit of scrambling to see over it, but what I found was encouraging. The garden of the house was heavily wooded—lots of places for a snoop to hide.

This was something I was used to—furtive lurking in gardens had become a bit of a specialty of mine. I clambered over the wall and began heading closer to the house. The ground was soggy underfoot but at least the rain had stopped. The house was huge—well over a hundred years old and festooned with rampant, out-of-control ivy. It was on three levels, in granite, with a massive frontage of bay windows and a genuine Victorian conservatory off to my right.

I'm no botanist, but all the trees in the garden had an exotic, almost foreign feel to them, and various large statues dotted the grounds, like people frozen at a garden party. Whoever Durban was dealing with was obviously well off—very well off. Durban's old Rover, although stylish, was the least expensive car in the drive. From my vantage on the wall I could see at least two Bentleys and a Porsche.

The driveway gates were still closed and there was no sign of movement in the gardens. I decided to take my chance and move even closer.

It was at times like this that I wished I had some toys—devices to listen through windows, tracker bugs, all that James Bond stuff—but there wasn't usually much call for it in the West of Scotland. I made my way slowly through the bushes, trying to get as close as I dared to the front of the house. I could see light ahead of me, so I got on my hands and knees and crept closer. By parting a few rhododendron branches I could see in through the bay windows.

It looked like a cocktail party was going on, one of those sedate country house parties of the kind I never got invited to. The average age of the guests was somewhere around seventy and none of them seemed to be enjoying themselves very much.

At first Durban was the only one I recognized but the rest of them looked similarly well-heeled and there must have been several tens of thousand pounds worth of jewelry on show.

Just then the fur-coated lady walked into view. She was giggling behind her hand like a schoolgirl, and the action suddenly made her younger, almost skittish. The smile on her face stayed with her until she walked out of my sight. It almost made me want to be in there with them.

The party seemed to be revolving around someone sitting in the corner of the room, just out of my sight. When the unseen person spoke, everyone else listened—a rapt expression on their faces, a mixture of deference and something else. I thought that maybe it was fear, but then again that might have been just my imagination.

I found a handy tree to lean against where I had a partial view of proceedings. I skidded on the damp bark, adding a new stain to my raincoat but eventually settled myself in and tried not to think about cigarettes.

It looked like I could be in for a wait. I contented myself with trying to guess the occupations of the people I could see.

There was the slim, suave, older man, a bit like Durban, but more ostentatious—silk handkerchief in the top pocket, suit from Saville Row, Rolex watch, gold cufflinks and diamond tiepin. Someone from the city? No, more probably an Edinburgh lawyer—there was something in his eyes that spoke of power. He had thin, almost feminine lips, and when he spoke he ran his tongue over his teeth as if savoring every word.

To his left there was a dowager duchess—all black lace and red silk, her hair pulled back severely into a bun, pince-nez poised delicately on a thin blade of a nose, top lip pulled down to hide protruding teeth. Her eyes were rheumy and ran with tears, bright sparkling droplets which were wiped daintily away with a small, black lace handkerchief.

I had her pegged as the widow of a country gentleman—one of the riding-shooting-fishing set.

Just at her shoulder there was the nouveau-riche businessman, looking out of place in such company. He had already drunk too much—I could see it in the reddening of his cheeks and the too careful way he had of picking up his glass. His suit nearly fitted him, and his tie was loud and garish. He laughed too much, and too loudly, but he didn't notice the disapproving looks he received from the others. Definitely a car-salesman, or a garage owner. I guessed the Porsche might be his.

And then there was Durban himself, completely at ease, one leg casually draped over the other, eyes watching everything in the room as he took delicate sips from his whisky glass.

The party continued at its own sedate pace, the unseen person stayed hidden, and I waited. Waiting is something you get good at in this job, and I had developed numerous mental games to keep my brain from going to sleep. I was working out the cube root of some ridiculously large number when things started to move and I had to pay attention.

The party began to split up and a light went on in the adjoining room. I just caught a glimpse of a huge mahogany dining table before the drapes were drawn in both rooms. I hadn't noticed it, but it had begun to get dark. As I looked up to the sky I felt the first spots of rain on my face. I debated returning to the car and waiting near the drive for the evening to end, but I had a feeling the festivities had yet to begin in earnest.

In the twilight I felt safe in having a cigarette, and as I smoked I could just hear the quiet murmur of conversation from the dining room.

I was there for another hour, up until eight o'clock, and was seriously damp by this time. The car was beginning to seem more and more inviting and I had just made up my mind to give up when a door opened at the side of the house and the party appeared.

I almost pinched myself to make sure that I was still awake. They were all robed, heavy black cloaks with pointed hoods, and they carried thick gray candles, hands cupped above them to protect their fragile sputtering light against the rain.

They walked slowly, sedately, and in the dim light it seemed that they were floating above the ground. I counted them as they made their way across the lawn into a heavier area of woodland—they numbered thirteen.

I got the cold shivers again—I remembered some of the stories from Dunlop's book and from the Internet—but I'd got five hundred a day, and that gave my client the right to a stiff upper lip. I followed at a safe distance.

We didn't have far to go. I reached a bend in the track we had been following and had just enough time to stop myself before I walked into a clearing.

It was a natural amphitheater, tall oaks surrounding a thirty-yard wide clearing. I noticed that great swathes of grass had been trampled down flat—this wasn't the first time they had done this.

Thick gnarled tree branches hung across the clearing, just above head height, branches that stuttered and twitched in the flickering candlelight.

They had arranged themselves into a loose circle. As one they bent to the ground, and at first I thought they were about to pray, but they only placed the candles at their feet. Their robes hung over their faces, throwing their heads into black shadow, and I had a sudden mental picture of the robes all falling to the ground, empty.

I had never felt more like running in my life. I had a cold, metallic taste in my mouth, and my palms tingled, pins and needles that seemed to dance just beneath the skin. If someone had put a whisky bottle in my hands at that point I believe I could have downed its contents in one, oblivion-seeking gulp. I tried to pull myself together and observe the action—that was what I was being paid for, after all.

When I looked back they were holding hands and facing inwards. One of them stood in the center—I couldn't see his face due to the darkness and the shadows, but I guessed this must be the one who had sat in the corner of the room. He started chanting and I could hear the foreign accent even through the incomprehensible speech.

Soon they had all joined in, but it still didn't help—I still couldn't make any sense out of it. It didn't sound like Latin; in fact, it didn't sound like anything I had ever heard. It reminded me of the harsh tongue of Mordor, but I couldn't imagine the well-heeled crowd in front of me as attendees of a Tolkien convention.

The circle broke, but only to allow one of the members to step into the center, before it formed again. A hood was thrown back and I saw it was the old lady from the petrol station. She took some papers from under her robe and held them in front of her. She started to read. Then she began to sing.

She was obviously a classically trained singer, maybe even an opera singer, but I doubted if the tune that came from her had ever been performed in any of the world's big theatres. It clashed in strange eerie discordance, running up and down scales that seemed first too flat, then too sharp. The air began to buzz around her, as if she was standing too close to a live power cable, and I think I saw the trees fade momentarily to reveal a greater darkness beyond, a darkness that seemed to writhe as if alive.

The song, if that's what it was, slowed to a deep chant, and the rest of the circle joined in once more. The chanting rose in pitch, becoming almost frenzied. The circle had begun to spin anti-clockwise, and I saw that they were all naked under the robes. I hoped it wasn't going to turn into an orgy—five hundred was not enough to make me watch this particular crowd in action.

It got cold quickly, and at first I thought it was only a night chill, but then I caught the smell—the dank festering odor that I'd noticed in MacIntyre's shop, and in my bedroom.

The circle stopped spinning and they all looked expectantly at the figure in the center. The figure there removed something from under his robes, and at first I couldn't make out what it was. Then I heard the noise—the pathetic, lost mewing of a small cat.

It struggled in his arms, but he had a tight hold. He raised it above his head in one hand, and I stopped breathing as the small creature fell quiet and still. He took something else from his robe—a thin, evil looking knife that glinted redly in the candlelight. With one fluid motion he gutted the small creature, first from chest to legs then across its body, letting its insides fall in hot steaming gobbets over his robes.

He stood stock still, hands still raised, and there was a moment of stillness. I realized I still held my breath and let it out slowly, noticing the small plume of steam as it hit the cold air. Suddenly he threw his head back.

The hood fell from his face and revealed a very old, obviously Arabian, man. Wrinkles ran like cracks across his face, deep fissures of black in the shadows. His teeth had all but rotted away, leaving only blackened stumps on the gums, and his nose was little more than a festering, rotting sore. But his eyes were alive. Clear, blue and shining as if with their own inner light.

He howled—a sound that shook the branches and echoed around in my head long after the actual noise had finished. A shiver passed across his face, like some small animal moving under his skin. He stretched. That's the best word I have for it, and I wish I didn't have to think of one. My brain was telling me to look away, but, like a car driver at a traffic accident, I couldn't take my eyes off him.

His head lengthened and broadened, becoming vast and red and pumpkin-like, putting out small bloody protrusions which burst like overripe fruit in a spray of gore, sending out blind, wriggling maggots which grew out like snakes, spreading fast, a multitude of them which writhed and crawled over his enlarged scalp. They flopped and quivered from his head in a seething mass, still anchored to his scalp.

Then he raised that gigantic, grotesque head, his eyes now blazing a deep, golden-red, and the tentacles stood around his skull like an evil halo.

Each tentacle had a mouth, and each mouth was full of silver pointed teeth from which a steady stream of saliva ran to glisten and bubble on the grass at his feet.

At the same time the old Arab's body flowed and melted. It was all I could do to hold in a gasp as I recognized the waspish waist and the bull-chest. Worst of all was the legs—they cracked and popped as the bones found a new structure and the creature bowed into a more crouched position.

Finally, the changes slowed and the creature pulled itself upright. I found myself looking at the living personification of the amulet, its black body gleaming like a well-oiled body-builder, its chest rising and falling as it took great, heaving breaths, the tentacles pulsing, mouths opening in time with its breath.

I realized that this was the murderer. I shivered involuntarily as I thought of old Jimmy, alone and defenseless against this monstrosity, struggling amid the organized chaos in the barn he called home.

The beast turned in a circle, arms outstretched, as if showing himself off to the audience—an audience which bowed in turn as his eyes met them. When he spoke it was in a deep bass register that rumbled across the clearing, and it vibrated in the pit of my stomach like a bass at a rock concert.

"SOTOTH ARAN PREDAK C'TENGI."
"KARAN F'THANG C'THULHU."
"IG SHUGGOTH NYAH."
"AMURAN ZOKAR NYARLTHOTEP?"

The last phrase sounded like a question. A tall figure stepped out of the circle to answer the monstrosity, and a conversation took place. I won't bother transcribing it here—I could make no sense out of it, anyway—but I recognized the tall figure as Durban. And as he talked, the tentacles still danced, the mouths gasping in time with the conversation, more silver ropy saliva dripping from the jaws to the dark grass.

Durban made an action with his hands, a strange fluttering movement as if performing a complicated shadow play, and the monster in front of him pulsed in and out of reality in time with the movements. Durban made one last pass of his hands and suddenly he was alone in the center of the circle. The smell was gone and I noticed the rain again.

The circle spun, singing in the same discordant voice, the chant rising, then rising again until its cadences filled my head and threatened to send me spinning along with them.

The trees themselves seemed to join in the dancing, and I was horrified to find that my throat tried to recreate their words. I had to shake my head hard and cover my ears before I managed to get some sense of equilibrium back, but even then the horrific singing seeped through my fingers, tugging at my mind, offering me treasures. It was sweet, it was seductive, but I only had to think of Tommy MacIntyre's body for the spell to lose its influence on me.

Finally, after what seemed like an age, the singing and the spinning stopped. The circle stood silent for long minutes, and again I had the impression that the hooded robes were just that—empty pieces of cloth that would at any minute blow away, screaming in the wind.

A collective sigh ran through the circle, and the crowd broke up. They headed back towards me and I only just managed to get behind a large tree in time.

They had split into three distinct groups led by Durban, and I caught some of his conversation as they passed.

"He was much stronger tonight " a female voice said. I think it might have been the duchess, and the measured tones that answered could only belong to Durban.

"Yes. Surely tonight he will find it."

I had to move closer to hear the next bit, increasing my chances of being discovered.

"This delay must not be allowed to go on much longer—it is nearly time. I told you we shouldn't have trusted Marshall. Men like him sell their Grandmothers to the highest bidder " someone said. From the tone of the voice I guessed it was the garage owner I'd seen before.

"You know we had to have a non-sensitive to do the job " Durban said. "Dunlop would have spotted anybody else too easily. Anyway—tonight should see the end of it."

"I hope so " the garage owner said.

"Are you doubting me?" Durban said, his voice suddenly full of menace. Again a chill ran through me. Durban was not a man to mess with.

"No. No.." the garage owner said, and dropped back away from the others.

"We are close " Durban said. "Very, very close."

They moved away towards the house, but I stayed under the tree, my mind spinning, trying to believe what it had just seen. I stood there until all the figures had gone back into the house and there was only the quiet dark and the sputtering rain.

The name registered… Marshall. I could almost hear the synapses connecting. I only knew of one

Marshall, Brian Marshall, burglar, rapist and all round bad guy.

I put the name together with the situation and realized what had happened. They had employed him to get the amulet, for reasons as yet unknown, but probably to do with the grotesque being I had just seen. And now he was holding out on them—just his style. And they had sent that thing after him. My only chance of recovering the amulet was to find him first.

I wasn't sure I wanted any further involvement in this case; it was getting just too weird for me, but as I've already said, five hundred a day buys a long supply of loyalty.

There was a rustle in the trees behind me, back in the clearing, but I didn't dare look round. Suddenly I didn't want to be there anymore. I made my way quickly back through the grounds, almost running, trying to ignore the flickering shadows which played on the statues, threatening to bring them to life.

The wall was wet and slimy after the rain and I managed to smear the front of my coat in thick green slime, but it didn't slow me down; I doubt if the Olympic high-jump champion could have gotten over the wall any faster.

My hands shook so much that I couldn't get the key in the car door. I stood there beside it, fighting for calm, smoking a cigarette down as fast as I could push it without bringing on a cough, waiting for my heartbeat to slow and my hands to steady.

I tried to rationalize what I had seen, trying to pass if off as a quicksilver conjurer's trick, but my mind kept going back to Tommy McIntyre, to the small bloody holes in his body, and those saliva-coated tentacles. The cold trembling in my spine stayed with me long after I finally got into the warmth of the car.

I drove back to the city as fast as the old car would allow. I planned to head straight home, but when I turned into Great Western Road I remembered someone who might help me find Brian Marshall.

I parked outside Wintersgills pub.

By that time I had calmed down. I no longer checked the rear view mirror every five seconds, my hands didn't shake, and when I looked in the mirror, I couldn't see the madness twinkling behind my eyes. The whole incident had taken on a strange, dream-like quality, but unlike a dream, it refused to fade from my mind. I still had difficulty assimilating it as a fact, but I had managed to distance it from everyday reality—far enough to stop myself being paralyzed in fear, anyway.

I had to be careful. Walking into a bar in my mood would be like playing Russian roulette. I was unlikely to come back out in a standing position.

I'd stopped here to pay a visit on Dave Knox. Dave and I went back to the time when I dropped out of University and he gave me a job behind the bar. I had stayed there for two years, completing the journalism correspondence course by day and serving the punters by night. I knew from experience that Dave had many contacts in the underworld and wasn't above more than a bit of dodgy dealings. I reckoned he would be as good a person to start with as anybody.

One thing I liked about Dave, he was always pleased to see me. The bar was quiet, only two old men and a dog in one corner and a small group of students in another.

"Derek " Dave said, and there was genuine warmth in his handshake. "Long time no see. What brings you to this corner of the jungle?"

"Oh this and that—you know how things are."

He studied me closely, and he must have seen something of the night's activities in my eyes because he poured me a whisky, which I accepted gratefully. His eyes widened as I downed it in one gulp. The hot burning nectar did a lot to dispel the coldness in my spine, but it still didn't erase it completely.

"Another?" he asked, but reluctantly I shook my head.

"No. I'd better not. I don't think I'm finished work for the night yet. Give me a beer."

While Dave poured the beer I lit another cigarette. This time my hands didn't shake.

We reminisced about old times for a couple of minutes as I sipped the beer, then I got down to business. He seemed surprised that I was interested in Marshall.

"A bit above your usual league, isn't he?" Dave asked, but didn't stop for a reply. "Actually, one of the lads was talking about him this morning. Marshall thinks he's hit the big time. Seemingly, he was in his local, boasting about how much money he had coming to him."

It sounded as if I was on the right track. Dave told me where Marshall's local was, along with a description of him, told me not to wait so long before my next visit, and offered me a free pint if I came back to tell him what it was all about.

The rain was coming down in sheets as I left, and I got soaked through on the way to the car. My aging windscreen wipers were barely up to the task and I had to take it slowly as I made my way across town.

Glasgow at night—what a city. The city center itself was quiet, but on the fringes the queues for the nightclubs were already building up.

Young girls, some no more than thirteen, teetered along slippery pavements in high heels, their bodies protected from the rain by pieces of cloth thinner than paper. Tattoos and piercing were much in evidence.

The males hunted in packs, and there were distinct tribes among them. First there were the gangster wannabes. From their dress you might have guessed they were from Harlem, but it took more than a gold chain, a shell suit and expensive trainers to look the part—Glasgow boys were just too thin on the whole.

Then there were the Sicilians. They'd watched too much American television. Smart Italian suits and shoes, designer sunglasses in all weathers and slick-backed hair was the order of the day here. Most of this lot would never get a girl—they'd be too busy preening in front of a mirror.

Then there were the tribeless—small pockets of kids, some with terrible acne and thick glasses. They wore check shirts and sensible pullovers over last year's fashion jeans.

They were only let out of the house on the condition they got home before eleven, and most of them were so drunk they couldn't stand. These were the dangerous ones, the unpredictable ones. They'd either start crying on you, or they'd pull a carpet knife from their pocket if you looked at them the wrong way.

I knew that predators would be at work in the queues—older youths, with the promise of a good time from pills, from sex, always for money.

Further out from the center other financial transactions were taking place. Hard-faced women of ages from fourteen to sixty stood on corners and waited to be picked up by men with warm cars and money in their pockets.

Amusement arcades glowed in blue and red neon as they fleeced coins from punters pockets, and bingo halls were beginning to disgorge little old ladies who's money had already gone.

As I got further from the center the traffic tailed off. The only sign of life was in and around the public houses. Kebab houses and chip shops were doing a roaring trade, and later, long- suffering Indian restaurant waiters would have to put up with drunks trying to prove their manhood by ordering the hottest vindaloo.

God, I felt cynical tonight. I promised myself that I'd take a holiday when this case was finished—somewhere warm, somewhere calm, somewhere that people didn't have to deal with ancient Arabians who turned into god-knows-what during magical ceremonies.

It was late by the time I reached the bar that Dave sent me to—a run-down, drinking man's pub in the East End, I just managed to order a beer before the barman called time.

"Just in time, son " he said to me. "But you'd better drink it quick—I'm shutting in five minutes."

It looked like it would be a lot longer than that—several of the punters had at least three drinks in front of them, but I suspected that they were locals, and well used to getting locked in, sitting in the dark, cradling their drinks and swapping stories till dawn. As an outsider, I wasn't to be privy to such activities.

The bar was full to overflowing with drunks, half drunks and not-yet drunks, and by the look of things smoking was compulsory. Not wanting to be out of place, I lit up and, trying not to seem conspicuous, looked around the room. I realized that Dave's description hadn't been thorough enough.

Shaggy black hair, blue eyes and a scar on the left cheek had seemed enough information at the time, but here in the East End scars were as common as acne on a teenager.

I started to think that my journey had been wasted until I overheard a shout across the room.

"Hey Marshall—have you made your million yet?"

There were raucous jeers in the far corner and I turned to see my quarry. Dave's description had been pretty accurate, but what he hadn't told me about was the temper—the flashing fury in the eyes.

What happened next was like a scene from a cowboy movie. Marshall stood suddenly, overturning the table and sending drinks and glasses crashing to the ground. With two steps he was standing in front of the man who had shouted.

Without saying a word he delivered the classic Glasgow kiss, a head-butt which hit his opponent just above the bridge of his nose, causing blood to spurt suddenly like a hastily shaken bottle of tomato sauce. The noise of the bone breaking was loud in the suddenly quiet bar.

Marshall stood over his prostrate opponent and drew back his foot for a kick to the head, but was held back by two men. The barman came round from behind the bar and shouted into Marshall's face.

"That's it! That's the last time. You're barred, Marshall. I don't want you coming round here again—understand?"

The violence was still there in Marshall's eyes as he spat in the barman's face.

The barman actually smiled, a huge grin, as he punched Marshall in the stomach, just once, but enough to knock the wind out of him, causing him to slump in the arms of the men holding him.

"You want to try that again?" the barman whispered, his voice carrying through the room. The hate in Marshall's eyes would have withered a lesser mortal, but the barman just snorted in disgust.

"Get that fucking arsehole out of here before I do him some serious damage " he said, turning away.

Still struggling, Marshall was frog-marched to the door. The prostrate man was helped to his feet, and the crowd returned to their drinking as if nothing had happened.

I finished my drink and followed Marshall out.

He stood, alone in the car park, and I saw the urge for violence in him. I made a play of lighting a cigarette as he lifted a dustbin and threw it against the wall, strewing rubbish into the street where it was caught and spun away by the wind and the rain.

"Fucking bastards!" he screamed, delivering a kick to the nearest car, leaving an obvious dent in its paneling before turning off down the street. A man of taste and charm, our Mr. Marshall.

I followed him, but it was risky business in the dark empty streets. Several times I had to duck into doorways to avoid being seen, and once or twice I got close enough to hear that he still muttered obscenities to himself. We went on for maybe a mile in this way, through tenement- lined streets as the rain pelted relentlessly down on us, until finally he turned up a path into one of the buildings.

It was an old Victorian tenement—four stories high and converted to flats. I knew the type. I'd lived in one similar in my student days. The close was dark and smelled of stale urine, and I'm sure I heard rats scurrying in the darkness as I entered. Five yards in I came to a flight of worn stairs. An unshaded light bulb lit graffiti-covered walls smeared in something that was brown and didn't bear thinking about.

From my position at the foot of the stairs I heard Marshall above me, still cursing as he climbed. I watched and listened as he made his way up to the top and heard the slam as he entered a flat before I followed.

As I climbed the stairs I tried to formulate a plan. Thus far I had been merely following my instincts and I had no idea how to approach him. I stood outside his door, still unsure, and lifted my hand to knock.

Before my hand reached it the door was pulled open and my arm grabbed tightly. He pulled me inside, hard, and as I tried to regain my balance, I tripped, falling face-first to the floor where the rough carpet scraped across my face.

I was roughly turned over and found myself looking into the angry face of Brian Marshall. I heard a harsh click, loud in the confines of the room, and caught a glimmer of silver as a flick knife was brought up in front of my face.

"And who the fuck are you?" he asked, the whisky fumes from his mouth threatening to engulf me. I was close enough to see every pore in his skin, to count the pockmarks from youthful acne scars. It suddenly struck me that he was afraid. Afraid...and very, very angry.

"You don't look like the Polis. Did they send you—the rich bastards wi' their plummy voices and their fur coats?" He didn't give me time to respond. "Did they?" he screamed in my face, and I felt quick lancing pain, then the hot rush of blood against my neck as he drew the knife through my left earlobe. I saw the smile on his face as he did it and I knew then that I wasn't going to be able to reason with him.

He shifted his weight and sat on my chest. My muscles tightened as I tried to breathe. He brought the knife up again and it headed for my cheek.

"All that talk of theirs about money—they didnae tell me that it was worth a fortune, did they?"

He was talking to himself, but I didn't have time to pay much attention; the dancing silver knife in front of me hypnotized me.

"Two thousand pound, they said. Bollocks—that wee trinket must be worth tens o' thousand, at least. And I suppose they sent you tae get it aff me? A saft bugger like you?"

He laughed, an evil, cold thing, and drew back the knife to strike.

I got my left arm in front of it. The blade sliced easily through my coat and the jacket underneath before bringing a burst of red heat as it found my skin, then my muscle. It scraped as it hit bone. I squirmed, trying to get some leverage, and tried to fight back the pain as I pushed, twice, before I managed to overbalance him. He fell away off my chest and onto the floor beside me.

I tried to scramble away but he was on his feet again before I had got off my hands and knees, and his foot drew back. I turned away, too late, and the booted foot hit me full in the ribs, sending me rolling into a corner of the room. I looked up into his eyes as he came for me and saw the wide grin. He was in his element. The knife glistened redly as he brought it up in front of him and licked the blade.

"Got you now, you fucker " he said and moved in for the kill. I tried to put my arms up in front of me but my chest muscles screamed in pain and refused to allow any movement. I kicked out with my feet, every action bringing fresh pain to my chest, but he danced away. He laughed again and waved the knife at me.

"I think the auld folk will hiv tae send somebody a wee bit bigger the next time " he said. He kicked me, hard, in the big muscle of my thigh, bringing another bolt of pain that threatened to send me spinning away into a faint. I struggled to keep alert, pushing my back against the wall, trying to get as far from him as I could. It wasn't going to be far enough—he was still smiling as he came for me.

I caught it, that fetid smell which stuck in the back of my throat. Marshall must have smelled it as well. He stopped, a puzzled expression on his face, then turned away from me as a rustling in the corner of the room caught his attention.

I followed his gaze, and my heart gave a lurch. Once more I had difficulty drawing breath, but this had nothing to do with the searing pain in my chest—this was from a much less physical source.

At first there wasn't much to see—only a deepening of the shadows, a new blackness that hadn't been there before. Then there was a spiraling, rainbow cloud of dancing motes of light that slowly coalesced into form.

Suddenly, the smell got stronger, enough to make my eyes water and my throat clam up in rebellion. The motes swirled faster, and a figure formed in the cloud, pulsing into and out of the blackness. There was the far off, almost inaudible, noise of flutes—no tune, no recognizable harmony, like a group of kids at their first recorder lesson.

I blinked, and it was there—the tentacled beast. It took full shape as I watched, drawing the heat from the room as it came through. A spider web of frost crawled its way across the mirror behind the creature.

"What the fuck is that?" Marshall shouted, looking to me for help, but I was only able to shake my head. Suddenly I felt pity for the man.

He turned away towards the door, but it was on him in less than a second, pouncing across the room like a cat after a mouse. It didn't seem to have any use of its arms; they hung, useless slabs of meat at its side. But then again, it didn't need them for its purpose. The tentacles all screamed in unison as it bore down on the doomed figure of Marshall.

The tentacles caught his arms first, and I could see the cloth of his jacket fray and tear as the tiny teeth went to work, saliva glistening evilly in the dark.

He screamed, in pain at first, then a loud roar of defiance, and lashed out with the knife, drawing a line through the red distended scalp of the thing. Blood welled up, but only for an instant—the wound closed itself almost as fast as it was formed. A shiver ran through the scalp, but the creature didn't falter in its attack.

Marshall opened his mouth to scream again, and one of the tentacles cut off the sound before it could escape, its saliva-coated teeth biting down hard on the meat of the doomed man's tongue, causing a sudden explosion of blood to run down the man's chest as the tentacle chewed.

More tentacles found his body; writhing and cavorting like a nest of snakes. One found his left eye socket and Marshall gave one last moan as it burrowed. His body jerked, once, then was still. The dead body was lifted off the ground and shaken like a terrier with a mouse, and there was a thud as something heavy hit the floor.

The creature lowered Marshall's body and bent over it, paying no attention to me as I started to scramble away.

All I wanted to do was to get out of that room, away from the horror, but my eyes kept drawing back to what was happening on the floor. I could see bulges moving from the mouths, down the tentacles towards the head, the large red raw head growing even as I watched. If anything, the noise was worse, the tearing and the gnawing sounding like a dog with a juicy bone, and, beneath that, a low, almost orgasmic, moaning.

I got myself to my hands and knees. Fighting back the nausea, I crawled towards the door.

I got halfway there when my hand struck something on the carpet. I thought at first it was the knife, but then I felt the grooves and the chain. I almost laughed—it was the amulet— Marshall had it in his pocket all the time. I wrapped the chain around my hand and kept going, the pain in my ribs and my arm causing me to wince with every movement.

It seemed to take forever to cover that short patch of carpet. At every moment I expected it to come for me, my back muscles tensed against the awaited assault.

My mouth wanted to scream, but I managed to force it down as I concentrated on reaching the door.

I only looked back once; as my hand closed on the handle of the door and I pulled myself upright.

Marshall's body lay on the floor, strangely deflated, and at least twenty tentacles still burrowed their way deeper, seeking out the soft parts, their slimy bodies red with gore along their whole length, the saliva now a pool on the floor, a spreading puddle of spittle and gore in which the creature knelt as it continued feeding.

I opened the door, slowly and very carefully, but I couldn't prevent the old hinges creaking loudly in the silence. The creature stiffened, and two of the tentacles lifted from their bloody feeding, dripping more gore and saliva onto the body beneath them as they swayed in the air like mesmerized cobras.

Although there was no sign of eyes, I had the feeling that they were watching me as they danced in synchronized time, tiny tongues licking their gums as if trying to taste my position. When another two joined them I knew it was definitely time to leave.

I ran out of the door fast, slamming it shut behind me, and got halfway down the first flight of stairs before the door shook as something heavy tried to force its way through.

Despite my pains, I ran faster than I had ever thought possible, my feet splashing through puddle after puddle as I made for the car.

I knew that I would be next—that thing wasn't going to stop until it had what it had come for. I'd run out of options—my only hope being to return the amulet to its owner and hope that she knew a way to stop the beast from taking it back to Durban.

I didn't pass anyone on the streets in my flight to the car—not even a curtain twitched at my passing. If someone had asked me to run a mile before that night I would probably have told them that I wasn't capable, but the adrenaline pumped through me and fear kept me going. I didn't look back, not once; I was afraid of what I might see.

The car park was deserted and the pub lights were out when I reached the car. I found my keys at only the second attempt and slid into the driver's seat, placing the amulet in the glove compartment and shutting it in where the sight of the tentacles couldn't remind me of the horror in the flat.

As I turned to reverse out I caught a flash of movement in the headlights and my heart missed a beat, but on a second look the beams lit up a startled cat leaving in the opposite direction.

Now that I had stopped moving I was acutely aware of my wounds and my pains. I felt the hot trickle of blood at my ear and my arm pounded with a dull hot thud in time with my heartbeat.

I couldn't go home, not when I knew that the creature had been there before, but I needed to do some work on the wounds, and I needed some rest. Suddenly I felt very tired. I thought of the people who would help, then remembered my promise to Doug. Maybe the archaeologist could help me make some sense of the situation.

Twenty minutes later I pulled up outside his house, and for the first time in a while I looked at my watch. It was only 12:30, only just over an hour and a half since I'd walked into the East End pub, only four and a half since the summoning in the clearing. It felt like a year.

Five

I leaned on the doorbell for long seconds as the tone played 'Amazing Grace'—a birthday present which Doug had found gloriously tacky.

I was jumping at shadows, half expecting the beast to pounce from the shadows at any moment. I held the amulet under my jacket in my right hand, as if keeping it hidden would somehow fool the creature that was searching for it.

Doug wasn't answering. I leaned on the door and banged it hard with my fist, sending a fresh jolt of pain up my arm. If he didn't come soon I would lie down and sleep, just curl myself up in his doorway and let oblivion take me down.

Suddenly the door opened, almost propelling me down to the carpeted hall floor. I managed to steady myself in time, bringing a fresh jolt of white pain to my arm.

"God, you're a mess " Doug said as he pulled the door fully open. His hair was splattered over his forehead in long strands, and I realized, for the first time, that he was going bald. He wasn't wearing his glasses and his eyes looked wide and naked, still gummy with sleep. I had got him out of bed, but I didn't have the energy to laugh at his Mickey Mouse pajamas.

"Aye " I managed to say. "But you should see the state of the other guy."

I almost fell into his arms, and he had to grab my arm to stop me from heading once more for the floor.

"Jesus Christ, Derek—what have you got yourself into this time? I..."

His voice drifted away. I looked up to find him staring at the object I held in my right hand—the grotesque shape of the amulet.

"Is that it?" he whispered, and I heard the awe in his voice. His eyes were big and round, like a kid on Christmas morning.

"Right first time " I said. "Just get me inside and you can fondle it to your heart's content. I even promise not to get embarrassed if you get a hard on."

He put out a hand to help me and I howled as he grabbed my arm right beneath the wound.

"For fuck's sake, Doug—be careful " I managed to moan when the pain had died down enough.

Sorry " he said, looking as if he might burst into tears. I gave him my other arm and together we stumbled into his house.

I tried not to drip blood on his carpet as he led me through the hall into his small kitchen. I had a bad moment when he peeled off my coat and I thought I might pass out, but the nausea receded, and I leaned against Doug's kitchen cupboards as he helped me take off the bloody clothing.

I'd have to rethink my image. The coat was a bloody, streaked ruin, and the jacket underneath wasn't much better. There was a sharp intake of breath as

Doug slowly stripped the remains of my shirt from the wound.

"Christ, Derek—I don't know where to start " he said, and there was doubt in his eyes.

"Just get on with it. You're the one with the first aid certificate."

He muttered to himself as he went to get his box of tricks.

"One week's training and I'm supposed to be a bloody expert."

His voice was raised as he called back to me. "Help yourself to the whisky. I think you're going to need it."

I managed to drag myself over to the cabinet above the fridge. I knew that's where he kept his booze; it was usually my first port of call. And one thing about Doug—he certainly knew his whiskies. I had a choice of six different malts. I poured myself a large glass of Talisker, hoping that its fiery heat would dull the pain enough, and slumped down in a battered chair.

The first sip burned on its way down, but the second went down easy, and so did the third. I was on my second glass by the time Doug returned with an armful of bandages.

I didn't feel too guilty about drinking it—after all, I'd bought the bottle in the first place, in return for some information on a previous case.

He looked worried as he put the bandages on the table in front of me.

"You really need a doctor " he said.

"At this time of night?" I said, "Do you know any doctors that'll come out after midnight?"

"Then we could take you to A&E at the Royal Infirmary. We could be there in half an hour?"

"No, thanks. They'll smell the whisky on my breath, assume I've been in a fight, and leave me sitting in a chair for a day or so. Come on, man...show some backbone."

He sighed deeply to show that he wasn't happy. He poured himself a whisky and sank a large gulp.

"I'll start with the arm first—that looks like the worst. I think your ear will be okay—it's only a nick " he said.

It might be only a nick to him, but it throbbed with a wet red heat, and it was all I could do to keep my fingers away from it.

"Talk to me " he said. "Tell me what happened tonight. It'll take both our minds off what we're doing."

I sipped whisky as he bathed the wound in my arm, and I told him the story. As I talked his gaze kept drifting to the amulet, and his expression ran the gamut of awe, disbelief and disgust.

"What, a real kitten?" he said as I got to the appropriate point. He suddenly looked pale, as if he might faint. Doug was a sucker for small furry animals. Give him a man with a festering hole in his arm and he'd patch it up with barely a qualm, but show him a kitten in distress and he turned to jelly.

"Yeah, a real one " I replied. To spare his sensibilities I glossed over the actual method of the cat's demise, but I didn't leave anything else out.

The story took a while in the telling, with interruptions for yet more whisky and questions.

"Run that bit by me again " he said when I had finished the story and he had finished bandaging. "The bit about the chanting. Could you repeat the words exactly the way you heard them?"

I tried, feeling at second hand the chill in my bones I had felt on first hearing them—even the air around us seemed to grow colder, as if the heat was being sucked out of the room. I looked up to see Doug nodding.

"Yes, I thought so. Don't go away" he said, and left the room at a hurry. I sat and drank some more of his whisky. I wasn't about to follow him…I'd had enough rushing about for one night, enough for many nights to come.

He came back several minutes later, cradling a book in his large hands, almost reverential in his handling of the old tome. The cover of the book crackled and whispered under his fingers, and I found myself hoping that he wasn't going to open it. He whispered when he spoke, as if afraid that the book might hear him.

"This is a modern transcription and commentary on an old medieval grimoire. It was originally written by a mad Arab, Abdul Alharazed, and it has to do with summoning creatures to do your bidding."

"What kind of creatures?" I asked.

"You don't want to know. Listen to this" he said, opening the book and reading. Strangely, his reading voice was a deep, bass register, reminding me of Orson Welles in his more solemn, self-important moments.

"Out beyond the stars they lived in blackness and chaos until the galaxies whirled into position and they came to walk the earth. The chief being of the mythos is C'thulhu, a god from beyond the stars, a once and future ruler of this planet. He walked the Earth many eons before man, and the ground trembled at his passing. He sleeps in Ryleh, his dreaming city beneath the seas, and when the stars are right he will awaken and chaos will once again walk the Earth."

He looked up at me and dropped me a slow wink.

"Good stuff, eh?" he said before continuing.

"The followers of C'thulhu have always been with us, from Atlantis to Mu, from Lemuria to Babylon, but perhaps the zenith of his priesthood came in Sumeria. The Sumerians inherited the lost wisdom of Atlantis, and were able to access the power of the Elder Gods through certain amulets of power."

"These amulets gave them dominion over the lesser beings of the ether and allowed them to perform works of great magic."

He was really getting on to it now, his voice reverberating round the room. It suddenly struck me that Doug would have made a good preacher—he had just the right mixture of plausibility and naiveté. I forced myself to pay attention as he continued.

"It is said that many dark secrets lie buried in the sepulchres of Ur. Men have searched the sands for long years and come away with nothing more than sand and dust. The secrets of the ancients remain hidden, and it would be better for mankind if they stayed that way."

I think I laughed...it was either that or a sob. I felt too tired to know the difference by then.

"Come on, Doug. What is this shit? It's like something out of a bad horror movie. You can't expect me to believe it?"

It was only when I looked into his eyes that I realized he was serious—serious and excited.

"How else do you explain what has been happening to you? I think we should keep an open mind until we get a better handle on it."

And this from a reputable scientist, no less. It was time to put him right on a few facts of life.

"I've got no intention of getting a handle on it. I'm going to get this little beauty here back to its rightful owner, then I'm going to forget all about it."

He actually looked disappointed.

"Come on, Derek. These are real bad guys we're talking about. I thought that was your thing. Besides…the amulet belongs in a museum, not in the hands of some private owner who probably never looks at it."

God, I hated his idealism sometimes. I took another long gulp of whisky before replying, noticing with some dismay that I neared the end of the glass. I started to feel a pleasant buzz. Not enough yet, but I was working on it. Another couple of glasses and it would be a head dive into welcome sleep. I summoned up enough energy to get the words out.

"As far as I'm concerned he's welcome to it—the less people who see it the better. And yes, much as I like to smack the bad guys on the chin, this particular bad guy doesn't have one. Besides, I'm way out of my depth here. All this Twilight Zone stuff pisses me off—you know that."

I'd touched on a subject that we'd argued about in the past. Doug had always been an old hippie at heart, always willing to believe any old crap.

As for me, if I couldn't eat it, drink it, hit it or fuck it, I didn't want to know. I realize that as a philosophy of life it was pretty basic, but it had got me through—at least until yesterday. Now I wasn't so sure.

The sooner I got rid of the amulet the better. I certainly didn't intend spending a night in the company of the thing. Taking my whisky with me, I weaved my way to the telephone, managing not to hit any walls on the way.

The phone was answered immediately, and although it was again the early hours of the morning, Mrs. Dunlop didn't sound tired. There was something in her voice, a subtle draining of emotion, an inflection that told me that things weren't all well in the Dunlop household.

"Do you have it?" she asked. No preamble, just straight to the point. I decided to follow suit.

"I have it " I replied, then waited to hear her speak again. I could easily have fallen in love with that voice, and the more whisky I drank, the better it sounded.

"You'd better bring it to me now " she said. "Things are getting a bit out of hand."

I snorted down the phone at her.

"You don't know the half of it. I've got bad guys coming out of the woodwork—and I mean right out of the woodwork."

There was a long silence at the other end of the line, a silence that went on so long that I thought we might have been cut off. But then finally she spoke, and this time there was a certain wariness in her tone.

"I take it things have been getting a little strange?"

That was an understatement if I'd ever heard one.

"Yeah, more than a little." I tried to keep the tremor out of my voice, but didn't quite succeed.

"I think you would be safer here with us " she said. I didn't see how they could help, but I didn't argue with her. I would be safer just about anywhere.

She gave me directions as to how to find her, somewhere out of town near the Campsie Hills, and asked me to hurry.

"I don't think we have much time " she said. I didn't understand what she was talking about, but even over the telephone I could hear the fear in her voice. I hung up on her this time, but I couldn't take any pleasure in it.

I returned to the kitchen to find Doug scanning the pages of the book.

"Does this look familiar?" he asked, and showed me what he was looking at.

The bad thing for my peace of mind was that it did. There, in a woodcut from the twelfth century, was an exact representation of the tentacled creature, perfect down to the pumpkin head and the sharp pointed teeth. It stood in a clearing in a thick wood, and in its tentacles it held a collection of small woodland animals, each of which had been speared by one of the razor- toothed mouths.

It gave me the creeps just to look at it.

"It's known as the Gatekeeper " Doug said. "It is supposed to stand guard between this world and the ethereal dimensions beyond. But there doesn't seem to be anything else about it. Do you want me to look further?"

He was as eager to please as a puppy, but I'd had enough for one night. I leaned over to close the book and, as I did so, the tentacles wavered on the paper, and the great head turned, only a fraction, towards me. I sat back abruptly, almost spilling what little whisky I had left.

"Close the damn thing, will you " I almost shouted. "I've seen enough of that monster to last me a lifetime."

Doug shut the book and put it down on the table in front of me. I reached over and pushed it further away—it gave me the creeps. Doug stroked the amulet, a far-away look in his eyes.

"You know, nobody really understands where this thing came from originally. It certainly wasn't made by the Sumerians. The old books say that it's over twenty thousand years old. If I could just get it back to the University, we could run some tests on it, find out exactly when and where it was made. It would be a sensation, a world-wide sensation, if we could prove its provenance."

"Down, boy " I said. "You don't want to be famous, do you? Fast cars, loose women and cocaine parties?"

"You mean move to California, catch some sun and laze around a swimming pool, drinking Tequila all day?" he said.

Actually it didn't sound so bad put like that, but I wasn't tempted. The sooner I delivered the amulet, got paid and got back to a life of unrelieved tedium, the better. I took the amulet from him.

"I'm afraid the owner needs it back rather urgently."

After I told him of my proposed trip to the Campsies, Doug was adamant that he was going along.

"You've had far too much whisky to drive. Besides, if that thing turns up again, I'll be along with the book. There's several incantations in there for protection against the old ones—one of them might work."

I certainly laughed this time. "I don't think a few bits of paper are going to stop this guy " I replied, but he was right about the whisky, and I was grateful for his company.

"Just one thing, Derek: if we're going visiting, I think a change of clothes would be in order, for both of us."

I looked at him in his Mickey Mouse pajamas, and he looked at me with the bloody remnants of a shirt hanging from my shoulders, and simultaneously we burst out laughing. I could almost feel the tension drain out of me.

Doug showed me to his wardrobe. Luckily, we were both about the same size, but that was about the only thing I was thankful for. Doug's taste in clothes left a lot to be desired.

He had never really outgrown childhood, and the wardrobe was full of sweatshirts, denims and sneakers. I picked the least offensive sweatshirt. When I pulled on an old leather biker's jacket I felt like a refugee from an American teen movie.

When I looked in the mirror I could almost have fooled myself that the night's activities had been a dream. Apart from a plaster on my ear, there were no external signs of damage.

My eyes told a different story—they had a hunted, harried look, and a twitch had developed on my left eyebrow. Small lines had sprung at the corners of my eyes, deep furrows that I'd never seen before, furrows which I wasn't going to be able to pass off as laughter lines.

"Hey, Doug?" I shouted. He arrived in the doorway, partially dressed, one leg down a pair of tartan jogging trousers.

"How old do I look?" I asked.

"Oh, about eighty " he said. "In a good light."

I cuffed him lightly with my good arm. He overbalanced, tried to right himself, failed, and tore a hole in the seat of his jogging pants as he fell over.

"Just as well " I said. "Any man who visited Artie Dunlop wearing those would deserve everything he got."

We took his car. It was capable of more than fifty miles an hour, which mine wasn't, and it was waterproof, which mine wasn't. The rain had got heavier, if anything, and by the time we left the relative shelter of the city it washed in sheets down the windscreen.

Doug kept up a constant flow of drivel to do with Elder Gods from beyond the stars, strange sects who met in dark woodlands and called up ancient evils, and some old sci-fi writer called Lovecraft. I had long since tuned him out.

I wondered whether I qualified for another five hundred due to it being after midnight. I also wondered how long it would be before I got to sleep in my own bed after an alcohol-free day. After the sights I'd seen I thought it might be a while yet.

My mind gave me pictures from the day—the police station, the 'duchess', the ceremony, and the East End pub. It kept skirting round and round the scene in Marshall's house—the pictures bubbling to the front only to be pushed back down again. I didn't want to think too much about Marshall, and if I could forget him and his fate completely I wouldn't miss it one bit.

The whisky I'd had in Doug's flat began to take effect, and I had trouble keeping my eyes open. The heat of the car and the murmur of the rain on the roof soon lulled me into sleep.

I dreamed of pizza. Huge pizza the size of tabletops—tuna, anchovy, black olives and pineapple topping, with a side helping of garlic bread, a Caesar salad, and a portion of French fries.

I was jolted awake as the car came to a halt. I had been salivating, and tried to discreetly wipe myself clean as Doug pulled on the handbrake.

"Wake up. I think we're here " Doug said, shaking me awake. I tried to peer through the rain but all I could see was a gravel driveway and the black, lowering shadows of the trees on either side. My mouth felt gummy, as if the small hairy creatures from earlier had crawled back in and died while I slept. The wound in my arm throbbed in time with my heartbeat, and even breathing hurt due to the kicks I'd taken in the ribs.

"I need a cigarette " I managed to mumble, fumbling my packet out from the deep inner pocket of the leather jacket.

"Yeah. Me, too " said Doug.

We lit up, neither of us with steady hands.

I noticed that he had the old book in his lap, and that his left hand was now curled around its spine, so tight that his knuckles had gone white.

"So what do you really think about the amulet?" I asked him as I puffed gratefully on the Marlboro, finally beginning to come awake.

"You mean, out here, in the middle of nowhere, with the dark wind howling and the trees writhing in the rain? At the moment I think you're right: the sooner we get shut of it, the better. It doesn't feel right. Let's just get rid of it so we can get home and demolish the rest of the whisky. Okay?"

I was in complete agreement. I wound down the window and flicked the smoldering butt of the cigarette out into the rain. I opened the door, wincing as the wind and rain swept in and the cold hit me. I put one foot out of the door, and it was on me before I had time to react.

The combination of cigarette smoke and wind must have stopped the smell from getting through before, but now my nostrils flared in disgust. The first thing I felt was a jolt as a tentacle lashed across my face, the tiny jaws zipping past my eyes, just missing taking my nose off as they snapped shut with a disappointed squeal. The rest of it came through into full solidity.

I found myself looking into a nest of writhing, chittering tentacles that swayed and danced in a forest around my head. Before I had time to react I was caught by the shoulders by at least four tentacles. They dragged me completely out of the car, kicking and squealing.

Doug screamed at the top of his lungs behind me. I felt like joining in, but the fear had almost paralyzed me, my heart felt tight and the screams bottled up in my throat. The tentacles parted and the great red head was revealed in all its gory glory.

I knew that somewhere in the depths there was a pair of scarlet, burning eyes, but they seemed to be covered in convoluted folds of raw, steak-like meat which squirmed as if a horde of maggots was squirming underneath the skin.

It pulsed, and the mouths on the tentacles screamed in rhythm as I got hauled closer to the main body. I hit out at the head, as hard as I could, and felt the flesh squash and buckle under my fist. It flowed and melted, beginning to crawl over my knuckles, and I just had time to pull my hand back before the flesh engulfed it. I left behind a large indentation in the head that seemed to fill with red, viscous blood before it flowed back into position.

The tentacles at my shoulders gnawed at the material of the jacket. I said a silent prayer to the god of black leather—it seemed to hold off their assault, for now, anyway. The beast lifted me higher and my feet left the ground.

Two of the tentacles waved in front of my eyes, hypnotic and enticing. The tiny silver teeth gleamed wickedly, and a long, forked tongue slithered and squirmed inside each of the mouths. They targeted themselves on my eyes, and moved closer.

Suddenly the thing dropped me to the gravel. I hit it hard and earned myself a new burst of pain from my damaged arm. For several seconds all I could do was lie there gasping, sucking in the rain.

Doug stood on the far side of the car. He held the amulet above his head and had the book open in his other hand.

"Barak klendor ig-nylauh prantan."
"Ia C'thulhu, Ia Sototh"
"Karam Ig F'thang"

The chant rang through my head, and the legs of the thing buckled as it made for Doug. It didn't go round the car—it climbed over it, giving me a perfect view of its hindquarters.

Down there, amongst a matted mess of pubic hairs, two tiny tentacles, no more than six inches long, waved and swayed in the wind.

The long talons on its feet scratched deep gouges in the bonnet of the car as it pulled itself over, closer to Doug.

I tried to push myself upright, but I had forgotten about my bad arm—it gave out under me and I fell back to the gravel.

"Cylar kornat trantom Ka"
"Karam Ig F'thang"
"Karam Ig F'thang"

Doug shouted through the rain, and time seemed to stand still. The amulet flashed blue in his hand, an almost blinding glare that seemed to freeze the creature on top of the hood. It raised its head and screamed, a howl that shook leaves out of the trees above us and threatened to chill the blood in my veins.

I almost cheered as the tentacles pulsed in and out of reality. I could make out the shape of the house beyond through the rapidly disappearing body of the creature.

"Get the fucker!" I shouted to Doug, not realizing that I was laughing.

But I celebrated too early. Still fading, the creature fell on Doug and tentacles grabbed him at the arm and waist. He looked over at me, the fear big in his eyes. He didn't even have time to struggle before fading along with it, his body becoming almost translucent.

A tentacle entered his cheek, slowly tearing a strip of flesh into ribbons and sending a gout of blood out into the night. His body faded down into transparency and I heard him scream, a long fading howl as they faded for the last time. I heard a thud as the book hit the gravel, but the amulet was gone, taken with them.

I crawled round to the spot where they had been.

"Doug!" I shouted, but there was no reply.

I picked up the book, hoping to find something, an incantation or a spell, which would bring them back. But the rain blinded me, and the water ran across the pages, leaving the text as a rippling blur. I tossed it away from me in disgust.

I think I could quite happily have stayed there in the rain, screaming my frustration and rage and pain into the gravel, but a hand on my shoulder stopped me.

I turned and looked up into the sad blue eyes of Mrs. Dunlop.

"I'm sorry, Mr. Adams. We weren't strong enough to stop it."

I noticed that she had already picked up Doug's book from where I'd thrown it. She helped me to my feet and began to lead me towards the house, but I wasn't ready to go just yet.

"Bring him back. You know something about this mess. Bring him back."

I realized that I'd screamed at her, only six inches from her face, but she didn't flinch, and, if anything, her eyes looked even sadder.

"I'm afraid we can't do that. We just don't have the power...not at the moment, anyway. You had better come inside. I think Arthur and I have some explaining to do."

I closed the car door after retrieving my cigarettes, and had to fight to suppress a sob. Doug was gone, and I had got him into it. Another friend had asked me for help, and once more I'd let them down. I wasn't going to be able to forgive myself, but someone, or something, was going to pay for this night's work.

The rain pelted down again, and I got soaked, but I stood for long seconds by the car, looking at the gouges on the bonnet, remembering.

"Just stay alive, Doug. Just stay alive till I get to you " I whispered, and had to shake my head. For a second it seemed as if he had answered, his voice screaming from a great distance:

"Help me. Help me."

I stopped and listened, straining at the edge of hearing, but there was only the wind in the trees. Dunlop's wife was already on her way back to the house, and I finally followed, hunched over against the rain.

The house was a huge, ancient, crumbling pile, all sandstone and ivy, and once into the hall it was like stepping back in time. The walls were hung with tapestries, old worn pictures of long forgotten battles. A grandfather clock stood imperiously in the corner. I'm no expert, but I would guess it was at least three hundred years old. Interspersed among the tapestries were ancient weapons, well worn, glistening with the patina of old age: claymores, muskets and pikes.

I half expected to come across a suit of armor or a bearskin rug, and wasn't surprised to find a rack of cabinets containing, amongst others, a stuffed otter and a very old badger with a sad case of mange.

I dripped water across the thick pile carpeting as she led me further into the house and showed me into a large room. The floor had been stripped bare, revealing shiny, varnished floorboards.

The second thing that caught my eye was the fireplace. It stood almost eight feet tall, and the blaze in the grate would have done justice to many a Guy Fawkes celebration. At that moment all I wanted to do was curl up in front of it and fall into the blackness of sleep, but I didn't think sleep would come, not for a while yet. Doug's screams still rang in my ears. There was more weaponry on show around the walls, and enough hardwood fittings to keep a small rain forest going. But more than that, there were the books—rank after rank of fine leather tomes in fine mahogany cases.

It was only after my gaze had circled the room that I allowed myself to look at the center, at the thing I had been avoiding. Some sort of diagram had been drawn out on the floor—a large circle with a five-pointed star inside. At each point of the star there was a candle and a small incense burner sending blue smoke up to hang in a heavy sheet in the still air.

The outside of the circle was inscribed with some indecipherable script, reminding me of Hebrew more than anything, and inside the circle, propped up on a bed of blankets and cushions, was Arthur Dunlop.

He wore a dressing gown that was faded and ragged with age and looked at least three sizes too big for him. It was only when I looked closer that I realized that he had once been a much bigger man.

"Sit down, Mr. Adams " he said, and his voice was weak and throaty. His skin was tinged yellow and his lips were almost black. He looked like a man who didn't have much longer to live. I opened my mouth to reply, to vent some of my pent-up anger, but he spoke first.

"I'm truly sorry about your friend " he said, but he didn't look sorry; he just looked sick. I suddenly felt angry—angry, confused and pissed off with this whole case. All I wanted to do was to get myself home, eat three pizzas, roll into bed, and sleep for a week.

"Sorry? Is that all you can say? Just what the hell is going on here?"

He coughed before he replied, and I'm sure there were flecks of blood on the handkerchief he used to wipe his mouth.

"'Hell' is the operative word, Mr. Adams. I'm afraid we have brought you close to its gates." He actually grinned at me as he said it, and I had to fight to stop myself shouting. This gangster was patronizing me. I was cold, I was wet, and I still didn't know what had happened to Doug.

"Maybe if you had told me how dangerous that trinket of yours was I would never have taken the case. Maybe…"

He stopped me with a wave of his hand, a small movement, but enough to bring on a fresh bout of coughing.

"No time for recriminations. I have a story I need to tell, and I think you need to listen if you are to have any chance of seeing your friend again. Now sit down. Please."

I sat in a huge red leather armchair, and his wife brought me a whisky. She left to stoke the fire in the large fireplace and I watched her move as the man started speaking.

He looked over at me. "Help yourself to more whisky at any time " he said, motioning towards the bottle on a table in the corner of the room. "We have a long way to go. I'm sorry if it seems over elaborate, but it is all pertinent to your problem."

I was puzzled. The man in front of me didn't seem like my idea of a gangland boss, but then again, I had never knowingly met one. Maybe they were all as cultured as he seemed.

I couldn't reconcile this man with the stories I'd heard. But, no matter how sick he was, if he had caused Doug's disappearance, or been involved with Wee Jimmy's death, I intended to see that he got put away for a long time. All I had to do was figure out how to make Stan and Ollie believe me.

I realized that my mind was wandering—a combination of the night's activities, the whisky and the comforting warmth of the fire.

"This is rather a long story, Mr. Adams. It might be better if you slept first—you look done in " Dunlop said.

"You don't know the half of it " I said. "But I've got a feeling we don't have time. Just tell your story. I'll try to take it all in."

Dunlop started talking but my brain was finally beginning to shut down. He told his story, and it seemed that I relived it in my head, in vivid, dream-like pictures.

I was looking into this self-same room, through the keyhole, and I was fourteen years old.

Andrew Dunlop was angry, no, more than angry, he was almost incandescent with the kind of rage that only teenagers seem able to manage.

His father had returned from the desert a whole two weeks ago, and so far Andrew hadn't been allowed to see any of the finds, let alone touch them. It was as if he was still a child, as if he couldn't be trusted with the exhibits. He was reduced to eavesdropping, creeping around in corridors, all the time trying to sneak a look at the treasures he knew to be there. Father would weaken, given time, but Andrew couldn't wait—he'd waited for long months while Father was away, and he didn't see why he should wait any longer.

Which is how he came to be peering through the keyhole into his father's study, crouched in a painful stance by the door, ready to jump away if he should be discovered.

Father had a visitor, which was in itself unusual—he was normally a solitary man, preferring the company of his books. What's more, he seemed to be arguing, his voice raised to a hoarse shout—a first in Andrew's admittedly limited experience.

The man he was arguing with was a good six inches taller than his father—a huge, fierce, proud man with jet black hair swept back from his forehead and deep, blue, piercing eyes. Andrew had never seen him before, but he knew this man must be Johnson.

He strained to hear the raised voices through the thick wood of the door.

"You must let us see it!" his father was shouting. "It belongs to everyone—not just to you. You've no idea how important this thing is."

Johnson was smiling, a strange, almost feral grin.

"And what if I told you I had no intention of letting it go, that I have every idea how important it is?" he said, his voice soft. Andrew was suddenly, for no obvious reason, frightened, and he wanted more than anything to leave, but something kept him there, crouched behind the door.

His father's voice was louder than before when he replied.

"I'll fight you Johnson!" he shouted. "I'll take it to the authorities! I'm sure they'll agree with me."

,Johnson's voice was almost too low for Andrew to hear, and he seemed to be talking to himself.

"Yes. I'm afraid they would. Which is exactly why I can't allow it."

A sudden chill swept through the keyhole, and Andrew was surprised to find that the door was cold to the touch when he pressed against it. He had to cover his mouth and nose with a hand—the smell suddenly threatened to choke him. His eyes watered, but he managed not to sneeze or cough.

Johnson started to speak, almost to sing, a harsh, foreign, almost animal sound. Andrew saw his father's eyes widen—in surprise at first, then in fear.

Suddenly it smelled even worse, as if something had died in the room, and his father's eyes were drawn to something in the corner, something out of Andrew's line of sight.

His father stepped forward, out of Andrew's view. Then the screaming started—a high- pitched keening that Andrew was unable to associate with his father. All he could see was Johnson laughing a great booming laugh as the screams went on and on before finally being cut off in one last, fading, echoing wail.

Nothing moved in the rest of the house. Andrew was waiting for someone to investigate, then he realized that there was probably no one else around. Mother had gone shopping, and Mr. Brown would be too far out in the garden to have heard anything.

Andrew couldn't wait any longer—he threw open the door, ready to protect his father, and was nearly knocked over by the departing figure of Johnson. The man didn't take any notice of him, merely swept passed and out of the house before Andrew had time to react.

His father's body lay curled, strangely small in one corner of the room, his hands curved into claws in front of his face, claws which hadn't been able to help him. His eyes were open, and red, bloody tears ran from their corners. Apart from the prone body, there was nobody else in the room.

His father's stomach had been opened, almost chewed, in a red gore-filled hole. A pool of blood was still spreading around him. Andrew sobbed and stepped forward, just as his father let out a small, almost imperceptible, cry of pain.

Andrew knelt and cradled the old man's head in his lap, unable to prevent the hot tears that ran down his cheeks.

The old man spoke just before the end.

"The amulet " he said, blood spattering from his mouth to join the pool on the floor. "You must get the amulet. Johnson will use it only for his own ends—it is a great evil that must be stopped."

Andrew nodded, and bent to move some hair from his father's eyes, but the old man was already dead. A wet mist clouded Andrew's vision, and there and then he vowed to have his revenge on Johnson.

The scene shifted, and Andrew grew older. And in every frame he was pouring over old books, books of ancient magic, always reading as his body filled out. Lines appeared on his features and his beard grew out into a long gray, flowing thing more befitting an Old Testament patriarch.

I jerked awake. Dunlop was still talking, but he stopped as I went over to the whisky bottle and poured myself another. I thought that if I had to go through twenty-four hours without food, I might as well get some calories into my system.

It took twenty long years as Andrew grew to manhood, grew to have enough strength for his challenge. He devoted his life to following his father in the study of mythology, but where his father had only harbored an academic interest, Andrew became a practicing magi, a master of ceremonial magic. He traveled extensively, and in his notes he tells of visits to occult schools around the world. He joined the Golden Dawn, and the O.T.O.

During the same twenty-year period Johnson's wealth had grown and he was now a very important man. He lorded it over Glasgow society, throwing wild parties that were famed for their debauchery. The press loved him, for his larger-than-life persona and his sense of style. They called him The Glasgow Capone.

Andrew followed his enemy's progress with great avidity, and was even more interested when an ancient Arab began to be mentioned in some of the reports.

He knew that the time was getting near—he had been studying the stars in the ancient eastern manner, and they all told him the same thing… a great ceremony would soon take place.

He began to pay even closer attention to Johnson's activities, and when a gathering was announced at Johnson's highland home, Andrew made sure he was an uninvited guest.

Andrew traveled to a remote part of the Highlands, to a dark, brooding house perched on a rocky outcrop above a raging sea. It was a stormy, windy night, wind lashing through the winter skeletons of the trees and black clouds scudding across the face of the full moon.

The coven had already gathered in the house, and Andrew was able to slip into the grounds without notice. He could feel the sleeping power in the place, the sense of doom hanging in the air, and he knew that he would have to be quick—the time was very near.

He slipped into the house through a patio window at the back. It had been locked, but locked doors were little problem for Andrew—his physical skills had grown apace with his magic, and he was an adept burglar.

The faint sound of chanting drifted up from beneath him. He knew that they would be in some kind of cavern beneath the house; he had felt the ancient power there in the first glimpse he had of the house. His movements took on a new urgency—he didn't have much time. There was no guard in the hallway—Johnson was too sure of his own strength, too cocky. Andrew intended to make him see the error of his ways. He was smiling as he made his way down into the depths of the earth, the chanting ringing louder in his ears as he descended.

The coven was in a circle, with the amulet on an altar in the center. There was no sign of the old Arab, but Andrew knew that he would be in the area somewhere—he was needed for the ritual. He suspected that Johnson was about to do a bit of showing off for his acolytes— summoning the amulet's beast into existence for their pleasure. Andrew smiled to himself. The ritual hadn't gone too far—he could still stop it.

Andrew strode into the center of the coven and, before anyone could move to stop him, lifted the amulet in his left hand.

The amulet seemed to squirm in his grasp, surprising him so much that he nearly dropped it. A sudden wind blew up, swirling and shrieking through the narrow confines of the room, strong enough to cause some of the coven to fall to the ground, weeping and wailing.

Johnson strode out of the crowd, making for the amulet, but Andrew held it away from the big man. Under his breath he was chanting a spell, an age-old protection, but he was suddenly frightened, aware that he might be out of his depth.

The wind dropped as suddenly as it came, and silence fell on the room, bringing with it the foul stink of the amulet's creature. Andrew knew it was time to leave, but his legs were refusing to obey orders, and he could only watch, stunned, as the swirling rainbow lights signaled the arrival of the old Arab—or whatever it was he had become.

Johnson began to laugh as the tentacles of the creature began to come through. Andrew hated the man, a deep lasting hate, and it was that hate which fuelled his next move.

He called up a spell from the grimoire of the mad Arab, one that had carried severe warnings against its use, but one that he knew he needed—it promised control of the creature.

Andrew felt the strength leave his legs, felt it flowing through him, and into the amulet. It burned in his hand, a deep emerald green, its glow throwing the room into dancing shadows, causing the coven to cower away from him in fear.

All except Johnson. He still had his eyes on the creature that had now fully materialized. He pointed a finger at Andrew and shouted one harsh, monosyllabic word.

Andrew enjoyed the confusion on the big man's face as the creature refused to do his bidding, and took even more pleasure in the fear in his eyes as the creature moved towards him, tentacles gaping greedily.

Andrew just had enough strength left to crawl to the cavern's entrance. He had one last look back and saw the creature leaning over Johnson, the coven watching on, too terrified to move. The last thing he heard as he made his way up the stairs was Johnson's dying screams. He was smiling as he made his way upwards, into the light.

At the top of the stairs he paused, holding the amulet aloft. He called once more on its power, realizing that he was draining something vital to his well-being, but wanting to finish it.

He shouted, his cry echoing around him like ghosts in the wind, and walls began to tremble. There was only one scream, quickly cut short, as the catacomb below collapsed in on itself in one long rumble of stone clashing against stone.

Smiling now, Andrew staggered out of the house into the clean, fresh sea air. And in his left hand, the green glow from the amulet pulsed strongly in the darkness.

I came fully awake with a start once more. I didn't spill any whisky though—some things are done on instinct. Had I been dreaming? Or was Dunlop's story still unfolding? In my befuddled state I wasn't sure, but I didn't have time to think about it as Dunlop continued.

Although he won the battle, Andrew was never to be a strong man again. He spent the reminder of his life writing down as much as he was able, leaving copious notes for the protection of his family against the amulet, and it's power. He died two years later, and although he was only thirty-six years old, his hair and beard were pure white and his eyes were the eyes of an old man.

Dunlop took another sip from the glass by his side before continuing.

"He was my grandfather. I never met him, but I have read all his notes, and followed all his advice. The care of the amulet fell on me, and I've done my best " he said.

I nodded noncommittally—I wanted to start playing things a bit closer to the vest until I really understood what was going on. The trouble was, I didn't think I'd ever understand this case—it was certainly different from my usual line of work, and I'd never complain about being bored again.

Dunlop was still talking.

"Since Andrew Dunlop died, my family has kept the amulet, binding its power with strong spells. Over the years we've tried to discover how to harness it's power properly."

"Don't tell me…John Harris " I said.

"My, you have been thorough " he said. "Yes. Poor John almost got us there. But his mind snapped, just as I was about to take control, and it slipped away from us again."

"Okay " I said. "I get that bit. But where does the gangster crap come into it?"

Dunlop smiled.

"I'm afraid I've got myself a bit of a reputation. But you see, my grandfather's notes held a great deal of esoteric information, and I have studied magic all my life. I know places to send people who cross me—

places where they'll never be found, places you wouldn't want to go to look for them."

"And the art thefts?" I said.

He waved his hand around the room.

"I have a lifestyle to maintain " he said. His smile reminded me of D.I. Hardy—they both had the same, cold certainty that they were right.

Dunlop continued. "There have been several attempts to steal the amulet by magical means, all of which we have been able to repel, but they mostly took place more than forty years ago, and my father had the task of dealing with most of them. I'm afraid I have been concerning myself with more worldly matters—not the least of which was marrying my wife."

It had been a relatively long speech for a sick man and he had to stop again as another bout of coughing hit him hard. A dark bubble of blood burst in his mouth before he wiped it away with a handkerchief.

"I'm afraid I have grown weak " he finally continued. "We didn't anticipate a human agency, especially after all this time—the burglary took us completely by surprise. I'm sorry that you got so deeply involved. Until two nights ago we thought it was just a common thief."

He lapsed into another fit of coughing. His wife went over and stood at the edge of the circle, a worried look on her face.

She didn't enter the circle though, even when the coughing got worse and he was forced to double up in agony on the floor, curled into a fetal ball.

She took up the story when it was obvious he wasn't going to be able to continue.

"Two nights ago, Arthur came under psychic attack from creatures from the Outer Regions."

She said it as if I was expected to know what she meant. I decided not to bother with questions at the moment—things were weird enough as it was. But there was one thing bothering me.

"So what was all that stuff about him being out of the country? Why didn't you fill me in from the start?"

She smiled for the first time that night.

"You were only told what was necessary—we didn't want to frighten you off the case."

I had to admit she was right. If there had been any hint of mumbo-jumbo I would have turned her down. She had used her beauty and wiles to make me help them. I smiled back at her as she continued, just to let her know I understood.

"He was only just able to fight them off, but it took most of his strength. Since then, there have been periodic attempts to get to him. He thinks he is being punished for keeping the amulet in hiding, and also being distracted from trying to find it again. But that's not the worst thing."

I wondered what could be worse, but again said nothing, contenting myself with sipping the whisky.

"The stars are right again, and we feel that an attempt will be made to call up the Old Ones. We need to know how you managed to find the amulet. You might know something important, and we must stop them."

It looked like it was my turn. I gave them the story, missing nothing out. I noticed a sharp intake of breath when I mentioned Durban, and another when I described the old Arab.

By the time I finished dawn was beginning to spread in the sky outside the windows and I felt tired enough to sleep for a week—no, make that two.

Dunlop spoke first, addressing his wife.

"We must stop them. It will be tonight, at the old place."

She nodded, and for the first time he stood, unsteady at first, then more confident as he stepped out of the circle.

"I think they will have more things to worry about than attacking me."

He turned to me.

"Do you want a chance to save your friend?" he said, and I replied instantly.

"If there's a chance. I got him into this, so I suppose I'd better get him out. But I've got a few questions."

He waved me aside.

"They will have to wait, I'm afraid. We must go to Arkham House...Johnson's old retreat. I'm sure that's where they will do it. We'll talk on the way."

He stood over me and took the whisky glass out of my hand.

"In the meantime, try to get some sleep—you look done in. It will be a few hours before we can leave. I have preparations of my own to make."

My mind was full of questions, but my body was dog-tired and the wound in my arm was throbbing angrily. Dunlop showed me up a huge flight of stairs and into a bedroom bigger than my whole flat. I didn't bother undressing; I fell flat on my face onto the soft sheets and was immediately asleep.

I dreamed, but not about food this time.

I was in blackness—deep, thick black. There was no up or down, only a never-ending sea of velvet softness.

Somewhere, Doug screamed. I made for the sound, aware that I could walk, but I didn't seem to be treading on anything solid.

I walked and walked and the darkness kept on going, and the screaming didn't seem to be any closer. Then, hours or days or months later, I caught my first glimmer of light and made for it.

Doug stood there, transfixed in a green flickering light that had no visible source. His eyes looked like black pits into hell as he turned to me.

"Help me!" he screamed, and reached out an arm. I moved forward to take his hand, and he contorted as a multitude of tentacles burst out of his body in a seething explosion of blood and fat and offal.

There were hundreds of them; swarming and chittering like a nest of demented snakes, and all with one purpose—to get to me. I could see the red lining of their mouths, could see the silvery saliva.

The first one came closer and I turned to run, but I seemed to be moving through black treacle, and the things kept gaining on me.

I managed one last look back at Doug's body to see the tentacles still pumping in a flood out of his deflating body.

The first of the tentacles caught me by the heel and began to chew.

I woke screaming.

Six

At first I felt disoriented, not knowing where I was.

The door opened, and Mrs. Dunlop was there.

"Are you okay?" she asked. "I thought I heard a shout."

My clothes were soaked in sweat, and at some point my arm wound had bled through the bandages, the sweatshirt and on to the sheet.

She, on the other hand, looked as perfect as ever. She wore a white cotton shirt and tight blue denims that looked like they'd been sprayed on.

I checked the time on the bedside clock—9:15--I'd slept for little over two hours, and it felt like it had been two minutes.

"Don't you ever sleep?" I asked her.

"Not recently " she said. "What with watching over Arthur and worrying about you, I've had enough on my mind."

"Worried about me?" I said.

She laughed. I could watch her doing that all day.

"Don't flatter yourself. We needed to find the amulet, and you were the best man for the job."

"Not good enough " I said bitterly.

I tried to push myself upright, and almost screamed as pain shot through my wounded arm.

She helped me up and out of the bed. I noticed her smell, and the strength of her body. I probably leaned on her a bit more than I should have, but infirmity does have some compensations.

"Thank you...what's your name, anyway?" I said. "I can't keep calling you Mrs. Dunlop—it makes you sound like one of my aunties."

"Auntie Fiona " she said. "I like the sound of that."

She led me through to a shower-room.

"Take that sweatshirt off " she said. "I'll go and get the first aid kit and have a look at the wound."

She left me in front of the mirror, and I had to hold onto the washbasin to stop the room swaying wildly from side to side. I let it steady down for a minute before peeling the shirt off and dropping it to the floor. I had a bad moment's panic when it seemed like my whole upper arm was just one huge, red wound. I took a sponge to it, carefully, and was relieved when the blood washed away to reveal skin underneath.

Doug's bandage was a sodden, soggy mess, and I peeled it off, carefully.

"That doesn't look too bad " Fiona said as she returned. I was acutely aware that my upper torso was naked.

"I bet you say that to all the boys " I said.

"My, somebody is feeling better already."

"Nothing a coffee, some toast, and a cigarette wouldn't cure " I said, as she efficiently rebandaged my arm. She made me flex the muscle to make sure it wasn't too tight, and pronounced me fit for action.

"Coffee's percolating in the kitchen " she said. "You'll find some fresh bread and cheese there as well.

The coffee's strong. Just follow your nose. I'll go check if one of Arthur's shirts will fit you."

"Make it white, if you can?" I asked. "And see if he's got a black tie I can borrow. I've got a funeral to attend." She raised her eyebrows, but didn't say anything.

I had another thought just as she was leaving.

"You don't have a picture of yourself in something skimpy, do you?"

This time her eyebrows almost left her face entirely.

"I don't think Arthur would like that " she said.

"I'm sorry to disappoint you " I said. "But it's not for me—it's a last favor for an old friend. An old, dead friend."

She must have seen something in my eyes.

"As long as it's for a good cause " she said. "I'll see what I can find."

She left me to find my own way to the kitchen.

The coffee was thick and dark. I found a loaf of bread, and the cheese. I think I ate half of both before my stomach and brain both decided enough was enough. The first mouthful of coffee caused my heart to race, and when I lit my first cigarette of the day I felt the caffeine and the nicotine fighting for control of my head.

Fiona came back and handed me a shirt, and a picture. In it she was sitting in a large armchair, one leg crossed over the other. She was much younger, her hair shorter and cut in a pageboy bob. She was also completely naked.

"Eh...thank you " I said, suddenly embarrassed. "Old Jimmy will appreciate it."

"Just don't let anybody else see it " she said, smiling. "If you do, I'll have to kill you."

She may have been smiling, but her eyes flashed. I didn't think I would be crossing her on this matter.

She handed me Doug's "grimoire".

"Your friend will want this back " she said. "And it'll give you somewhere to hide the picture."

I wondered if taking the picture was such a good idea. It only needed the wrong person to find it for the potential of blackmail to be huge. I almost handed it back, but the last thing that Jimmy had said to me was 'Remember the photo'. I'd ignored Liz's last plea—I couldn't ignore Jimmy's.

I opened the book to put the picture in...and got the woodcut of "The Gatekeeper" again. And again it moved, that great bulbous head turning, the small, beady eyes staring out of the book, straight at me.

"Avaunt!" Fiona shouted, and the book snapped shut in my hands. She took the picture from me and slipped it inside the book's front cover.

"You've got to watch some of those old books " she said. "They sometimes seem to develop minds of their own."

Five minutes later we were sitting in a conservatory drinking expensive coffee and watching the sun slant through the latest rain shower.

Arthur's shirt fit me perfectly—I'd been right about him once being a much bigger man.

Fiona handed me a black tie.

"Arthur would like you with us tonight at the Arkham House " she said. "And I agree with him. We need to leave here mid-afternoon at the latest."

"Don't worry " I said. "I'll be back in time. Arthur seemed to think that Doug is still alive, and if he is, I'm going to bring him back. I'm not losing another friend."

I remembered the dream that had wakened me, and I shivered, despite the heat of the sun.

She sat opposite me, her legs crossed, her hair falling around her shoulders. I thought about the picture she'd given me, and suddenly I wanted to crush her to my chest and hold her tight for a long time. There was a silence between us, then she smiled.

"Arthur will be up and about soon. If you need to go, I'd go now, before he tries to talk you out of it."

I nodded.

"I'll go when I finish this coffee " I said, raising the cup. "Just one thing, though...to fill in the blanks. Tell me about John Harris."

Her eyes clouded. There was pain there, an old pain. I recognized it; I'd seen something similar in the mirror often enough.

"Poor John. He couldn't stop. He was driven, an obsessive. We found him after his Hunterian Museum experiment. Arthur had detected movements in the ether."

There was a joke there waiting to be told, but I let it be and allowed her to continue.

"After that, Arthur funded his research. We knew he was on to something, and hoped that he would find a way to bind the power of the amulet. The night at Maes Howe was a culmination of years of work."

She stopped and sipped her coffee. She was far away, back in the burial mound.

"And it nearly worked. John took us to the 'veil', and we saw through it. Arthur wanted to send the amulet through there and then, to place it beyond the reach of anyone else. And he nearly achieved it. But something began to come through from the other side, something hideous and dark. The sight of it drove poor

John mad, and we lost control—almost lost everything—but between us, Arthur and I managed to repel the invader. We were unable to save John's sanity. He never recovered."

Tears ran down her face. I could have done something, offered her comfort, but I just sat and stared.

"And you paid his hospital bills?"

"Yes " she said, getting herself under control. "For as long as his doctors thought he needed them. We offered him a room here, and he stayed for a couple of months. But he was a wanderer at heart, and slowly he spent more and more time away, until eventually we only saw him maybe once a month."

"And when was the last time?"

"Just before the amulet got stolen " she said. "Maybe two nights before."

I wondered whether Brian Marshall had ever met John Harris. It would explain how the burglar knew precisely where to go. It was probably something I'd never know for sure—another loose end never to be tied.

I finished the coffee and rose from the chair.

"After the funeral, I'll come straight back " I said. "Then you can tell me where Durban fits into the scheme of things."

She nodded.

"Just don't be late. It's a longish drive, and it would be best to get there early rather than late."

She stood and waved me off as I drove Doug's car down the driveway. I looked in the rear- view mirror. It was the picture of the life I would never have—the big country house, the wife at the door waving me off to work. I felt like pounding the dashboard in frustration as I pulled out on the main road.

I thought I'd left plenty of time to get to Clarkston, but I got lost in North Glasgow. I stopped in a high street of a suburb I didn't know, and made the mistake of asking a kid for directions.

"Hey son " I said, rolling down the window. "How do I get to the city center?"

"Down the road, left, then left again " he said.

I thanked him, followed his instructions, and five minutes later found myself travelling back down the same high street again. The kid was pointing at my car and laughing. I slowed down and rolled down the window.

"Hey mister, are you wan o' the 'Blues Brothers'?" he said. "My mammy says they're shite."

The temptation to stop and pound the little shit to a pulp was high, but I fought it off.

"You're a genuine pillar of the community " I said. "You'll probably grow up to be a Tourism Coordinator."

He looked at me as if I was stupid. It was that generation gap thing again—it seemed there was nobody under twenty who understood me. I left him trying to catch flies in his open mouth.

The local newsagent had a street map, and I stood in the shop, tracing a required route.

"Are you going to buy that?" a shrill voice said. The shopkeeper advanced down the aisle towards me, her hands over her bosom as if she was afraid I might attack it.

"No. Why bother, when there's so many helpful folk in this town?" I said. I left her to catch whatever flies the kid missed.

It took me a couple more hours to get to Clarkston, then twenty minutes more to find a parking place. I ended up ten minutes walk away, and as I walked back towards the church, I was surprised to see Durban's Rover parked just outside the driveway.

I was late—the service had already started. To my surprise, the downstairs area was full— even the standing room. I moved upstairs, but even there most of the pews were taken. Wee Jimmy had known a lot more people than I imagined. At least I had a good view of proceedings.

Old Joe from the paper-shop was down near the front. His wife wasn't with him, though— after all, someone had to run the shop. Durban stood near the back. He had a solemn look on his face, but every time I looked at him, I saw the fate of the kitten, and the monster that had been conjured in the clearing. He saw me looking, and dropped me a slow wink.

Two rows in front of Durban, my attention was caught by a mass of long black hair. The owner of the coiffure turned slightly, and I saw it was Mandy, with a new wig. She had dressed demurely for the occasion— her boobs were nearly covered, and her skirt was halfway down her thighs. The man to her left stretched a hand round her shoulders and squeezed her close, but her expression never changed, and she didn't stop chewing her gum.

The priest stood above Jimmy's family, hands outstretched, appealing for God to take the soul into heaven. I have always found the idea of heaven, especially the Christian one, particularly distasteful—not enough fun, and too much piety for my liking. My personal prayer was for Jimmy's soul to find happiness wherever it had gone.

The prayer finished, the congregation muttered a ragged "Amen", and six of Jimmy's family, all small males with thinning hair, ages ranging from twenty to sixty, stepped forward to lift the coffin.

The organ began the funeral march in a loud burst of wheezing bellows, and a small procession led by the tall minister filed out into the sunshine. I gave them a couple of minute's start, then made my way down the stairs.

The sunlight was blinding after the gloom of the church, and it took my eyes a minute to acclimatize. I looked around for Durban and saw him entering his car. He waved to me, and his smile was broader than ever. I was about to follow him when a hand clasped my shoulder.

"It was good of you to come. Jimmy thought a lot of you, he always said you were his best friend—you always treated him like a human being."

I turned and looked into the face of John, Jimmy's oldest son, a small, quiet man whose eyes were filled with pain.

"I'm really sorry, John " I said, then realized I didn't have anything else to say—my mouth had gone dry. How could I tell this man that his father had most probably been killed by an ancient Arabian demon, and that even now the killers were plotting global domination by Elder Gods from a different time and space? In the cold light of day, it all seemed absurd.

Not for the first time on this case, I wondered if I was going mad.

I had stopped paying attention, so I got a surprise when Jimmy's son gripped my right hand, turned and walked away. I looked down. Sitting in the palm of my hand was a small, oblong piece of card. The side facing me was blank, but I didn't need to look to know that the other side contained a drawing of a small red coffin and a number. I had been chosen to aid in lowering the old man into the ground.

It was only when I raised my head that I saw the priest beckoning me across to join the other men clustered around the grave.

I stood on the left of the priest, both hands gripping white-knuckled on the purple ribbon. As the priest prayed, we slowly let our ribbons pass through our fingers, lowering the coffin into the dark black earth.

I had to fight to keep control of my end of the box. The pain was back in my arm, a deep, lancing throbbing that almost made me lose my grip. Somehow, I managed to cling on—I think it was the thought of the potential embarrassment if I failed that did it.

As the priest came to the end of the prayer, the pine box settled on the floor of the pit and a smattering of earth rattled across its surface.

The rest of the funeral crowd began to drift away to different corners of the graveyard. Jimmy's relatives got into the long black cars, shaking hands before leaving for the traditional round of tea and whisky. Soon there was only the priest and myself left, looking down at the coffin.

The priest turned away, but I stayed there for some time. I wasn't sure what was keeping me there, and I had no idea what I would say before I opened my mouth.

"I never really got to know you as well as I would have wanted to, but I hope that wherever you are, you're happy. And I promise you—I'm going to stop those who did this to you."

And suddenly I found myself crying. No tears, just great dry heaves that raked through my body. I wasn't sure whether I was crying for Jimmy, for John Harris, for Doug, or for myself, but when the sobs finally passed I felt a whole lot better.

I had Doug's book in the pocket of the leather jacket. I took it out, half-expecting it to be smoking this close to a church. I removed the photo of Fiona Dunlop with my fingertips without opening the book. Resisting an almost overwhelming urge to keep it for myself, I let it drop into the grave. Remembering a funeral from my childhood, I searched my pockets for small change. Finding a five pence piece, I tossed it onto the coffin, wincing as it rattled heavily across the brass plate directly above where Jimmy's sightless eyes must have been.

A flash of black and white sped from a tree on my right, swooped into the six-foot hole, and, as I looked on dumbfounded, the magpie hopped out, the coin firmly held in its beak. It turned one jet black eye on me and seemed to give me a long, slow wink; then, with a quick flurry, was once again airborne.

I had a feeling that Jimmy had just sent me a sign. Perhaps the supernatural was not all a bad thing. I left the graveyard with a slightly lighter heart than I'd entered it. The sun was shining, and the leather jacket suddenly felt heavy. I took it off and swung it over my shoulder, feeling the weight of the grimoire hit me in the small of the back. I caught myself whistling as I left the grave behind.

My newfound good cheer didn't last long—Newman and Hardy were waiting for me just outside the graveyard gates. I hadn't spotted them at the funeral, but they both wore black ties, and it looked like they had combed their hair. They were really pushing the boat out. I wondered if they had really known old Jimmy.

"We thought we'd find you here " Newman said.

"We wondered if you had anything new to tell us?" Hardy said.

My heart sank. I thought they'd found Marshall's body. I knew that if they had, I was in trouble. I had been seen in the bar, and I had been seen leaving just after him, and I was sure I must have left fingerprints all over his room.

"Come on guys " I said. "I've just buried a friend—can't it wait?"

"Oh, a friend, was it?" Newman said.

"And how many more 'friends' are you going to be burying?" Hardy said.

I had a sudden mental image of myself at Doug's funeral, trying vainly to explain to his mother how her son had come to die. I resolved that I'd do everything in my power to make sure it didn't come to that.

"And what do you mean by that?" I asked, trying to keep my anger at bay.

Suddenly I realized that they couldn't have found Marshall—they were being much too polite. If they had discovered the burglar's body, I would have been in the cells faster than I could blink. I began to relax—not much, though. It always paid to be careful where Stan and Ollie were concerned.

"Well?" said Hardy.

"Well?" said Newman.

"Well, what?" I asked, and Newman stepped towards me before being restrained by his partner.

"Well, have you remembered anything else?" he said, slowly enunciating every word, the voice he would use when talking to a school child. "Or are you too busy playing at detective to do any real work?"

"No. There's nothing else I can think of. Did you find out where that fancy leather outfit of Tommy's came from? I think that might give you a clue as to who killed him."

"We thought maybe you lent it to him " Hardy said.

"We thought maybe you were bum chums?" Newman said, and both the policemen laughed. I didn't join them—there was no humor there.

"No. There's no mileage in following the outfit " Hardy said.

"We've found out that he brought it himself, mail order " Newman said. "We found the receipt."

So Tommy had never intended the outfit to be sold. That didn't surprise me. I don't like to speak ill of the dead, but Tommy had been congenitally incapable of telling the truth, no matter how easy it would have been to do so. He saw it as a contest between himself and the rest of the world. I reckon the rest of the world won, in the end.

I suddenly had an idea, a way to get some more help on our side.

"Actually, I did hear something this morning. I was just going to follow it up."

I hoped they were going to buy it. If they did, it might slow our adversaries down and give us more preparation time.

"Remember that thing I was looking for?" I asked.

Hardy snorted, but Newman looked interested, so I addressed the rest to him.

"I've heard that Durban—you know, of Durban and Lamberts—I've heard that he's been putting out feelers, trying to find a buyer."

It had the desired effect. I'd played on the right prejudices. What more could they want—two antique dealers dead, and now a third involved in the case. I could almost hear their synapses making connections. The wrong ones, of course, but if it got them off my back and onto Durban's, I wasn't going to complain.

"I wouldn't bother following it up " Hardy said.

"Just leave it to us " Newman said.

"We'll check it out " Hardy said.

"You'd better be careful " I said. "That was three that time."

"What—"

"—was—"

"—three?" they said in turn. Then I got that smile again. I wondered how long they spent practicing together.

They had already walked away when Hardy turned back.

"By the way, Mr. Adams—how did you get that?" he said, pointing to my arm.

At first I didn't realize what he was asking, then I looked down.

My bandages had leaked. It must have happened when I helped to lower the coffin. There, in the crook of my elbow, was a still spreading stain of blood, an inch wide.

I tried to look casual, but I'm not sure I succeeded.

"I cut myself shaving " I said, showing him the plaster on my ear.

He looked closely at me, suspicious. I realized why when I ran my hand over my chin—it was obvious I hadn't shaved recently.

"Designer stubble " I said. "It's all the rage. I was just tidying it up a bit."

"Designer stupidity, more like " Newman said.

"Come on " Hardy said, as he turned away once more. "We can't stand around here all day."

Newman still studied me. He came closer and waved a finger in my face.

"You're up to no good, laddie. You know it, and I know it. So you had just better be careful. We'll be keeping an eye on you."

"Just the one?" I asked, and cursed myself inwardly. I could see that I'd gone too far. He stepped closer to me, so close that I could smell his cheap after-shave.

"That mouth of yours is going to get you into trouble some day " he said. He clenched his fist and drove it, hard, into my midriff, forcing me to double up. I almost expected a follow up blow, but when I looked up he was just standing over me, a look of sadness on his face.

"Now look what you made me do " he said. He waved his finger in my face again, but I forced down the urge to bite it.

With one last wave of his finger, he stomped off after his partner, leaving me to start breathing again. I realized that someday soon I would have serious trouble from that policeman, but at the moment I had more than enough other worries.

I had one last look back at the graveyard before I left. The men had started to fill in the grave, and some of the flowers were being blown away by the wind. The magpie was nowhere to be seen. I said a small personal prayer to Jimmy before leaving, hoping that wherever he was there were still Chandler books to read. If he was in the right place, he might even get to read a new one.

I drove back to Dunlop's house as fast as possible without exceeding the speed limit, and arrived to find Dunlop struggling out of the house with a suitcase. Whatever was in it was obviously heavy, but he refused my offer of help.

"And about bloody time, too " was all he said. "Help Fiona with the other case, will you— we're getting short on time."

I did as I was told.

Fiona was in the hall. She had changed into a blouse and skirt, and I thought I glimpsed, as she bent over, the tops of stockings. Did this woman not realize the effect she was having on me?

I helped her carry the case outside, and when I got back out I was just in time to see Dunlop loading the other suitcase into the boot of a large black Mercedes.

I found that I was nominated driver. Dunlop was clearly too ill to try, and Fiona couldn't drive.

"We'll take this car " Dunlop said. "Can you drive an automatic?"

I couldn't, but I wasn't about to tell Dunlop that. I was almost salivating at the thought of being in control of all that sleek, black power. I decided I had better put in a token protest; I didn't want to seem too keen.

"Wouldn't we be better off in something a little less conspicuous?" I asked, pointing over at Doug's car. "Someone might be watching out for your car."

"I don't think it matters much " he replied. "I'm pretty sure they'll be expecting us to try something. We may as well travel in comfort."

By the looks of him he'd need all the comfort he could get. I had doubts that he would survive the trip.

Dunlop got in the back and Fiona got into the passenger seat, her skirt riding up to show an expanse of thigh. I had been right about the stockings, and it was all I could do to keep my hands on the wheel. I know—all very childish, very macho, but show me someone who wouldn't have been moved by those legs, and I'll show you a woman.

I almost embarrassed myself just getting the car started, and managed to stall it twice before we even got to the road, but after a few minutes the car seemed to drive itself. It was silky smooth and purred like a big cat. On any other day I might have taken a great deal of pleasure from being behind the wheel.

The early part of the journey passed uneventfully. Dunlop had told me little more than to head for Fort William and points north. Fortunately there was only one road, so it was difficult to get lost.

"So tell me about Durban " I said.

"There's not much to tell" Dunlop said. "His great grandfather's name was Johnson. Does that tell you all you need to know?"

I did. I'd been right about the family feud.

The car was a joy to drive and the rain had eased. By the time we reached Loch Lomond, the sun poked its way through the clouds and I had mastered the controls. The scenery was at its best, with just a fine mist covering the hilltops.

We had been cruising along in silence for about half an hour before Dunlop spoke to me again.

"You seem to be taking all this very calmly, Mr. Adams. We must seem very strange to you."

I looked at him in the rear view mirror.

"Aye, strange is a good word for it. But I've seen too many 'strange' things in the past few days—I think I'm suffering from overload."

He started to laugh, then thought better of it as another coughing fit hit him.

"One thing does worry me, though " I said. "I just can't imagine you as the man who controls the North Side."

This time he did chuckle.

"Oh yes—I have my father to thank for most of that. But I like to keep my hand in. We all have some price to pay for our power."

Whatever that meant, it was too obscure for me, but I wasn't able to quiz him further. We got caught in a spot of heavy traffic and I had to keep my wits about me as the boy-racers played their games in front and behind me.

Once the traffic had calmed down, Dunlop started talking to me again.

"Tell me about the Arab you saw—what did he look like?"

I didn't have to think too hard; the image was ingrained in my mind. I described him, as best as I could, and when I had finished Dunlop looked thoughtful.

"Just as my great grandfather described him " he muttered.

I jumped at that, and almost lost control of the wheel.

"What do you mean—it can't be the same man. Can it? He'd have to be well over one hundred years old—maybe as much as fifty years over."

"Oh, it's the same man, all right. And he's much older than that. I wouldn't like to guess how old, but Great-granddad reckoned it might be as long as three thousand years—maybe even older. It is rumored that he is the same age as the amulet itself, and that could go back tens of thousands of years."

I think I snorted, but my mind was reeling. It was just too much to take in. I concentrated on the road while Dunlop continued.

"Whoever, or whatever, the Arab is, his life has been bound with the amulet and the ritual. Great-granddad speculated that he was one of the original priest kings, bound to walk the earth until the stars were right for the ritual. From grandfather's research, I think I have a fairly good idea of his motives. A long time ago he was the keeper of the amulet, but he abused its power and it was taken from him and placed in the sepulchre, surrounded by rock and bound by many spells. He was exiled, forced to wander the desert for centuries—you'd be surprised how often he turns up in old legends—until Johnson came along."

He paused and coughed up a lump of blood into his handkerchief. I only caught a quick glimpse as he put the handkerchief away, but it looked like a piece of raw meat.

I was grateful for the pause; it gave me a chance to check the rear-view mirror. We were being followed. I'd spotted the same car three times over the last fifty miles. They hung well back, and never came too close, but it was the same car, all right. I didn't tell my passengers; I didn't want to alarm them. Anyway, they must be police. It was just Stan and Ollie's style—they probably put the tail on me right after I met them at the cemetery.

I decided to ignore them. They might come in useful later on, but for the moment they weren't causing us any difficulty.

Dunlop was still coughing, and it was several seconds before he was able to continue.

"In Johnson the Arab found a man he could use, a man he could mould to his own ends. What with Johnson's ambition, and his dynamite, the old Arab got what he wanted—the amulet. If it hadn't been for Andrew, he might have achieved his purpose already."

I didn't want to ask any more, but he was bent on telling me.

"When the stars are right, and he has the amulet, then Great C'thulhu will be called from his dreaming sleep. That's what we are going to have to stop."

"And this C'thulhu chap? He's a bad guy?"

Fiona answered this time.

"One of the worst—he is the very embodiment of chaos. If the ritual is successful, C'thulhu will be able to reclaim his old form and all of evolution until now would be reversed in an instant—it would mean the earth being returned to its primal form."

"A bad idea, I think you'll agree, Mr. Adams " Dunlop said, and chortled again until a fresh bout of coughing forced him into quiet.

I talked quietly to Fiona for a while, but didn't learn much new. She thought that we had a chance to disrupt the ritual and retrieve the amulet. A slim chance, but one we had to go for. I got the impression she didn't expect to survive the trip.

"And where does Doug come into this?"

I saw her glance quickly at her husband, and he shook his head.

"We don't know " she said. "We hope that we will find your friend at Arkham House, but it may be too late."

I resolved to put my mind in neutral and go with the flow. I would keep my head down and let Dunlop get on with the hocus-pocus. If a chance came to save Doug, I'd take it. And if Doug could not be saved, somebody else would pay.

I'd paid already.

Dunlop slept for most of the rest of the trip, and after a while Fiona was keeping her thoughts to herself. Every time I glanced over at her she had her eyes half closed and she muttered to herself, but I couldn't make out the words. I contented myself with enjoying the feel of the car, and admiring the sweeping scenery.

Near Crianlarich I decided it was time for a cigarette. I needed some rest anyway—my arm had started throbbing again, and the stiff pedals were giving me shooting pains in my calf muscle. Dunlop was still sleeping, so we left him in the car.

Once I'd got my cigarette going I asked Fiona what she thought was waiting for us.

"Hell, Mr. Adams. Pure, unadulterated hell. Just pray to whatever gods you have that we get there in time."

"I don't believe " I said.

I realized I didn't sound convinced. If I had answered her just three days ago there would have been no hesitation, but something in the things I'd seen had got through my cynicism. I found that I couldn't cope with the idea of so much evil without a balancing force, a force of good.

She gave me the smile again, and I felt something melt inside me.

"You don't sound as if you're very convinced about that " she said, echoing my own thoughts back to me.

"I'm not, but I always fancied changing my mind on my death bed, preferably after my ninetieth birthday."

Now she looked serious, two small lines appearing as furrows.

"I just hope you don't have to do it sooner."

She accepted my offer of a cigarette and we smoked in silence for several seconds.

"So how did you get involved with Dunlop?" I asked, and she gave me more than a smile, she gave me the full works.

"You mean, what's a nice girl like me doing in a place like this?" she said, and I had to join her laugh.

"I met Arthur through the Craft " she said, and must have noticed my blank stare. "I'm a witch. Hadn't you guessed?"

"Where's the broomstick?" was out of my mouth before I could stop it. I thought at first she was angry, but then she threw her head back and roared with laughter.

"You really don't know anything about us, do you? It's not all libido-raisers and palm reading."

I had to admit she was right—films had clouded all my views on the occult. I learned fast, though. I found out a bit more when I asked her what she had been muttering in the car.

"Protection, a spell to keep us all safe. You won't have noticed, but we have been under psychic attack since we left the house. Only the combined efforts of Arthur and myself have kept them at bay. They know we are coming."

"Is there anything I can do?" I asked, hoping she wouldn't say yes.

"Just drive, and keep an open mind. I've got a feeling things are going to get a lot stranger yet."

A cloud swept over the sun and a cold shiver passed down my spine as I got back in the car. The first thing I did was check the rear-view mirror as I pulled out. Our tail was still there—they pulled out of a lay-by a couple of hundred yards back at the same time we started moving.

Dunlop was still asleep, new flecks of blood at his lips, blood that bubbled with every breath. I didn't say anything—the man's health was his own problem. I still hadn't made up my mind if I liked him. Oh, he was pleasant enough, but there was an undercurrent there, something somehow slimy and evil. After all, you didn't get a reputation like his in Glasgow without some cause. Mrs. Dunlop was another proposition entirely: I refused to believe that she was capable of any wrong, but maybe I 'd been blinded by her obvious charms.

The pursuing car fell in behind us. Now that we were out in the open road they found it more difficult to sit four hundred yards back. Once more I chose to ignore them.

"Do they work, then?" I asked Fiona.

"Do what work?" she said, puzzled.

"You know—those potions you mentioned—the libido raisers."

She laughed out loud at that one, again showing off the perfect dental work.

"What a quaint way you have with words. Of course they work." She gave me a little sideways grin. "Not that I've ever had a need for them."

"So, another stupid question for you " I said to hide my sudden embarrassment. "How did you get into all this weird occult stuff in the first place?"

She gave me the smile again. I wondered how many men had melted before it.

"You know, you're quite cute when you blush. I started young " she said. "I blame it on my grandmother. She was always doing weird things—reading tea-leaves, making up potions for women in the town to help their men along in bed—all that kind of thing."

"Later, at school, I got together with a group of friends to play with a Ouija board. That was the start of it."

I looked over at her. She was lost in memories. I decided to let her go on—I was actually getting interested.

"We got in touch with something, certainly, but even now I'm not sure what it was. At first the messages were obviously fake—one of us must have been pushing it. Then things started getting weird. I started getting personal messages, things only I knew, and they would come through even when I wasn't touching the glass. Most of the messages were spiteful, the sort of thing that hits teenage girls where it hurts. And whatever it was, it was powerful. One of the girls had a nervous breakdown, and I started sleepwalking. It was after I was found, five miles from home, wearing only a night-dress, that my parents took me to see a specialist."

"I bet you looked a picture " I said, before I could stop myself.

She gave me a tight-lipped smile, but didn't stop.

"The specialist happened to be a white witch—she had no great power, but she made up for it with lots of enthusiasm. She recognized something in me, and for the next two years, on the pretence of therapy, she taught me in the ways of the Great Mother.

"By the time I was seventeen I'd learned everything she had to teach me. I did some fortune telling to make some quick cash, and I began to visit other covens, taking part in ceremonies. It was at one of them that I met Arthur."

"What do you mean—covens?" I asked. I had the picture in my mind again, the thirteen hooded figures around the obscene, tentacled beast.

"Oh, you needn't be worried. There was no black mass, no devil worship—no sacrificing of virgins. No, this was the old Craft, the one that has been around far longer than the obsolete symbols of Christianity. Arthur was officiating at the ceremonies. You should have seen him in those days—a fine figure of a man, so strong, so confident."

She looked back at the man in the back seat, and her eyes were glistening with tears.

"So what went wrong?" I asked, almost afraid of the answer.

"Greed, Mr. Adams. Greed and the desire for power. Mr. Durban, whom you have met, has forged an alliance with the Arab. He lusts for the power that his great-grandfather was denied. Arthur has used all his strength in fighting him, and he has had to resort to some of the same methods. It has broken him."

She bent over the seat and placed Dunlop's coat over his sleeping body, as if looking after a child. I had a feeling I still wasn't getting the whole story. Dunlop just didn't strike me as a victim, but I kept my mouth shut; it would wait.

As she was turning back, her body went rigid and she let out a small cry of pain. I hit the brakes, but she stopped me with a hand on my shoulder.

"No " she said through clenched teeth. "Keep going. And don't stop."

I got the car moving again, and at the same time she started murmuring under her breath once more. The muttering was to continue for the rest of the journey. Somewhere north of Oban, Dunlop woke up and joined in as well—it was like sharing the car with a buzz saw.

I could see in the rear-view mirror that he was sweating, great heavy drops that ran greasily down his forehead. He wiped them away with the back of his hand, but never broke the cadence of his mutters. I drove for nearly two hours with the pair of them droning in the background. In the end I opened my driver-side window and tried to let the road noise drown them out.

I needed the window open for another reason—I felt dog-tired. I'd had maybe eight hours of real sleep in the last sixty. I'd pulled plenty of all-nighters in the past, but never on a case of this intensity.

The road got narrower and windier north of Fort William, and I had to concentrate harder. I opened the window further until the breeze was like a gale blowing through the car. I'd be using up a lot more fuel, but I wasn't paying. As I drove I smoked cigarettes—Dunlop didn't look like he would complain—and tried to keep my eyelids from drooping.

He finally made me stop the car near the new bridge to Skye. I deliberately waited for a blind corner before I stopped, and I had to brake hard to get us into the roadside parking place in time.

Ten seconds later our tail flew past. I had been looking forward to seeing the shock on their faces when they saw us at the side of the road, but I was the one who got the surprise.

I had expected some junior policemen, not Stan and Ollie.

And I didn't see any surprise. All I saw was Hardy's dour features staring straight ahead as they passed us and kept going. I had underestimated my importance to them—they must really have suspected me to follow me this far. Then another thought hit me—maybe it wasn't me they were following after all; maybe it was Dunlop.

I almost told Dunlop, then, hoping he would turn back and forget about the amulet. But then I thought about Doug, about my dream of the night before. I'd got in too deep to back out now.

We all got out of the car, and I wondered what was coming now. Dunlop looked even worse, and he had to hold onto the car for support as he moved round towards the boot.

"We're getting close. Time for some preparations" he said, taking the suitcase from the boot. I had to help him with it—he didn't seem to have any strength left. He asked me to put it on the ground.

"Turn away" he said. "You don't need to see this."

That was like a red rag to a bull. I did turn my back, but couldn't resist a peek over my shoulder. I soon wished I hadn't bothered. Luckily there was no one around—we could have been arrested on the spot if anyone had caught a look at the bag's contents.

Let's just say that 'portable abattoir' would have been a good description. There were bits of raw steak—large pieces of red meat floating in glass jars. I couldn't identify the cuts; I tend to like my meat already hidden in pies, but it didn't look like beef or lamb. One of the pieces looked remarkably like a penis, but I'm sure I was mistaken. I hope I was.

He took something red and dripping from one glass jar and deftly cut it into three segments.

"A little steak?" he asked, handing me a piece. "For strength."

He must have seen the disgust on my face.

"A little too raw for you? We can soon rectify that." He passed his hand over the meat and there was a sizzling and the sweet smell of cooking meat. Despite myself, I found that my mouth was wet with saliva.

"Eat it " he said, passing the now-charred flesh to me. "You'll need it later."

I took it gingerly and studied it while he passed the other piece to Fiona. I watched her reaction, and she didn't flinch before popping the piece into her mouth.

It certainly looked like steak. I took a bite and my mouth watered as I chewed the soft meat. It had a heavy tang I had never tasted before, but it went down smoothly enough.

"Good?" Dunlop asked, and I nodded assent. He smiled at me slyly, and I wondered what I had just eaten, but I didn't have the nerve to ask.

The sun was just going down behind the Cullins, throwing a pink sheet across the evening sky. A light wind sent white horses scudding across the surface of the sea. The hills stood out gray and stark on the skyline and somewhere overhead I heard the hunting call of a buzzard. Sometimes I wonder why I bother staying in the city. I resolved, when this was all over, to get out into the country more, to see more of my native land. I just hoped I'd have the chance to do it.

All three of us stood in silence for a while content to let nature take its course. Suddenly Dunlop and Fiona moved close together.

"Join us " she said, stretching out her hand.

I took it, and Dunlop took my free hand. It was like holding hands with a corpse—his palm was cold and clammy, somehow greasy. I felt self-conscious, half expecting a busload of tourists to leap out and start filming us. That all disappeared when Fiona started to sing.

It was soaring, it was melodic, and it moved me, bringing pictures of simple life in forests, of crystal clear waterfalls, of wildlife in abundance. You know the kind of thing—picture postcard scenery for tourists. But Fiona's voice overcame my cynicism, bringing surprise tears to my eyes.

It sounded like Gaelic, but I couldn't be sure. Dunlop's hand felt damp and heavy in mine, but I soon failed to notice. A tingling spread through me, like mild pins and needles that started at my feet and moved slowly up my body. It felt as if my hair stood on end, and I seemed to be drawing heat straight from the sun. The pain in my arm, which had been with me all day, faded to a dull ache then melted away completely. Beside me, Dunlop straightened and his skin color improved markedly. He still looked ill, but he no longer looked like he might die at any minute.

Fiona seemed to have grown in stature, and she had taken on an inner glow. The song finished but we stood there for several minutes, grinning at each other inanely.

Dunlop was the first to move.

"We are as ready as we can be. Time to go."

I had a mind full of questions, but Dunlop waved them all away. An hour ago he had looked near death, now he looked ready for anything.

"No time for questions, Derek, The stars are almost right. We must go; I have an ancestor to revenge."

As we got into the car I flexed my wounded arm, gingerly, expecting a flare of pain, but there was nothing, just a vague numbness. I pressed the wounded area lightly, but still there was no pain.

Fiona put a hand on my arm.

"Don't worry, Derek—I haven't harmed you. And it will only last a few hours. By tomorrow morning you'll have the pain back again, I'm afraid."

I put it to the back of my mind, aware that it was getting crowded in there with unanswered, maybe unanswerable, questions, but I forced myself to concentrate as Dunlop told me where to go next.

I was no longer tired. And for maybe the first time since the start of the case, I didn't want a cigarette. I'd have to ask her the secret of her song. If we could market it as an anti-smoking cure, we would make a fortune.

Dunlop directed me north along several single-track roads, hedges pushing in close to the car, trees overhanging in a huge, gnarled arc, almost blotting out the sun. I took it slowly, easing the big car round the corners, aware that at any moment a crazed tourist could be coming the other way, one who was doing at least sixty while studying a map.

Dunlop seemed confused at first, but then began to grow more confident, as if he was recognizing landmarks. He leaned over my shoulder and asked me to stop as we crested a hill overlooking the sea.

We were standing on a promontory, looking down to a small island about four hundred yards from us. White spray lashed the black rocks on the cliffs beneath us, and on the island, in the middle of a densely wooded area, sat a Gothic mansion straight out of an old Hollywood B- movie, something knocked up in a couple of days by Roger Corman.

The stone looked black in the last rays of the dying sun, twin turrets jutting skywards like arms reaching for the sky.

A whole horde of small protuberances stuck out from these turrets and, although we were too far away to be sure, I was pretty certain they would prove to be gargoyles.

A thin causeway led from the road, across to the island, and ended in a wide drive in front of the house. There were several expensive cars parked in the driveway, but I didn't recognize any of them—the policemen's car was not among them. I hoped we had finally lost Stan and Ollie, but in my heart I knew that they were around, somewhere, just waiting for the right moment to make their move. I hoped they would give me time to find Doug—if he was anywhere on this earth to be found.

I realized that I was probably going to be in trouble with the policemen when this was all over. Then again, a couple of hours of boredom in a police cell sounded fine just about then. I promised myself that I would never whine about being bored again.

Look where it leads you.

My mind was wandering again, trying to ignore what lay ahead. I didn't like the look of that house—I didn't want to go down that hill.

As we watched, lights winked on in two of the windows like giant eyes snapping open.

Seven

The island was made of solid rock and stood twenty-feet out of the water on dark basaltic cliffs, on top of which sat a wall that must have been ten feet high. The only entrance was across the man-made causeway to the imposing wrought-iron gates.

"Welcome to Arkham House " Dunlop said, and I half expected a bolt of lightning and a roll of thunder to accompany his words.

"And what now?" I asked. "I don't think any of us are up to climbing those cliffs. And they're not going to let us just walk up the drive. How do you plan to get in?"

He patted the side of his nose with his index finger.

"Trade secrets, I'm afraid. But it will be best if we wait till full dark—the ceremony will not begin until midnight, and the less time we spend in the house grounds the better."

"And then what?" I pressed, but I didn't get any answer. Fiona got out of the car, then back in again to sit beside Dunlop in the back.

"Could you leave us alone for a bit, Derek?" she asked. There was genuine pleading in her eyes; I couldn't refuse.

I left them in the car and went out to watch the last of the sunset. Stars were beginning to twinkle into existence overhead. I wondered what was 'right' about them on this night in particular—to me they looked as cold and impersonal as ever.

I looked back into the car, and looked away again quickly. They were in a clinch, like a pair of teenagers out on a date. I walked away and left them to it, but I couldn't help being jealous.

The road was heavily wooded all the way down to the island, but I didn't intend going any closer to that house until it was absolutely necessary. I walked back up the road for fifty yards, just far enough so that I could no longer see the couple in the back seat.

I lit a cigarette and tried not to think of how quiet it was, trying not to wonder what was making the noises in the undergrowth. The cigarette tasted burnt—a piece of dry ash—and I wondered why I had ever put one in my mouth. I stubbed it out on the bark of a tree. It was when I flicked the stub away that I spotted it.

It looked like a rear end of a car, the taillights still faintly burning, hidden behind a mass of gorse bushes.

I crept closer, having to push the thorny bush aside to get through, but soon, only ten yards from the road, I stood beside Stan and Ollie's car. They'd driven it off the road, then covered it in branches. I wondered if it was us they were following—after all, hadn't I put them on Durban's tail earlier. Maybe they were down at the house already?

Then I saw the blood. They weren't going to be bothering me any more...they weren't going to be bothering anybody any more.

I didn't want to look too closely, but I knew what had got them—the puncture marks from the tentacles were becoming all too familiar by now.

I tried to open the car doors, thinking that one of them might still be alive, but the doors were all locked, from the inside. I considered breaking in, but there was no need; it was obvious that both men were dead—very much dead.

The interior of the car was like an abattoir, crimson splashes of blood and gore across all the glass. The policemen were both in the back seat in a tangle of arms and legs, in a cruel parody of the loving couple in the car a bit further down the road. It looked like they had tried to put up a fight—and failed.

I did stay around long enough to check if their radio might be working, but I could see through the windscreen that it, and all the instrument panel, had been broken and smashed.

Just then there was a loud crack as something heavy moved in the undergrowth. Ten seconds later, I was back beside Dunlop's Mercedes, wheezing and panting as if I'd just run a mile rather than less than a hundred yards.

When I reached the car I looked back up the road, but nothing moved, there was only the quiet dark. I thought of how it must have come on them, silent and deadly and completely terrifying in the claustrophobic confines of the car. I shivered, and I wasn't entirely convinced it had been brought on by the cold.

I was about to rap on the back window, to tell them of my discovery, when I saw that Dunlop was asleep, his head lying in his wife's lap. I couldn't be sure—it was dark in the car— but it looked like she had a stream of tears running down her cheeks.

That was when I decided not to tell them. It would have to join the other matters awaiting the outcome of the night's work.

I lit a cigarette, by habit more than from any need, but the sight of Newman and Hardy had broken some of Fiona's spell. I sucked it down and concentrated on blowing smoke-rings for a while.

We'd have to put a codicil on that spell if we wanted to sell it: Not effective in the face of violent death.

I was on my third cigarette and beginning to get cold by the time the couple joined me, hand in hand like a pair of teenagers. I could just see the hands of my watch—it was 9:30.

"We have to time this right " Dunlop said. "We have to get into the crypt, and the best time to do that will be after they are all there. I'm betting that no one will want to miss the ceremony. We shouldn't meet anyone on our way there."

I was puzzled. "But you said they knew we were coming, didn't you?"

He patted me on the shoulder. "Oh yes. And they do. They have other means of guarding themselves. Which is why we must be prepared."

He went back to the car and came back with three glass bottles from the suitcase. I didn't look too closely at their contents. He put them in a small backpack that he struggled to fit over his shoulders. He took something else from inside a small black bag, but he was too quick for me. Whatever it was went into the backpack with the jars.

"A fine night for a walk " he said, and winked at me. For a man who was about to do battle with demons he was in a sprightly mood, but then again, I myself felt full of confidence and eager to get going. Even the sight of the dead policemen hadn't affected me as bad as I would have imagined. I suppose it was something to do with Fiona's spell—I had no fear, no apprehension. Maybe fear was easier than nicotine addiction to conquer by magic. That didn't surprise me much, given how hard I'd found it over the years to give up smoking. "I'm ready for action " I said. "Let's do it."

"Come on, then " Dunlop said. "We can't wait all night."

We made our way down the hill, watched all the way by those giant unblinking windows, and as we got closer the feeling of being watched got ever stronger.

I wondered what Dunlop had in mind. I couldn't believe that we would just walk up to the door and ask politely if we could get inside, and we certainly wouldn't get away with pretending to have a breakdown—some clichés were just too old to work.

Dunlop had got a few yards ahead of us and I took the chance to ask Fiona if she knew what was going on.

"Just stick with Arthur " she said. "He knows what he's doing."

The rest of the journey down the hill passed in silence except for the crashing of the waves on the rocks below. I could smell salt in the air and feel fine spray on my face. More than once I had a brief, regretful glimpse back at the car.

Dunlop stopped us again just before we stepped onto the causeway and led us out of sight of the house.

"It's time for some more protection " he said. He made some passes with his hands, and I was reminded of Durban's actions at the previous conjuration, but Dunlop's were slower, somehow more graceful. It brought to mind of the careful, slow movements of an old Chinese martial arts expert. It was almost hypnotic.

Suddenly his hand shot out towards Fiona and a shower of dazzling blue sparks flowed over her body, dancing in a spiral which wound around her body, faster and faster until she was almost blocked from view by the whirling light.

Dunlop shouted, one harsh word, and the lights froze in position. They winked once, and she was gone.

It had happened as suddenly as that. I believe I gave out a small yelp of surprise, but I couldn't be sure. I was almost too shocked to move.

I stepped forward, ready to grab Dunlop, believing some treachery, but was stopped by a chuckle, a female chuckle from my left-hand side.

"Don't worry " Fiona said, the sound of her voice coming closer. "Arthur knows what he is doing." I felt a finger touch my cheek and jumped backwards, suddenly afraid. I turned back towards Dunlop in time to see him point at me. My body tensed, expecting a blow that never landed. My sight was filled for an instant with sheeting blueness that seemed to fill my mind.

I blinked, just once, then tried to rub my eyes. I seemed to be peering through a fine mist, and at first I thought it was my eyes, but when I lifted my hand I saw blue, electric sparks dancing across its surface.

Fiona was back, her body pulsing in an aura of turquoise brightness. She laughed, a high- pitched, girlish giggle, and twirled with her hands outstretched, sending showers of sparks dancing from her fingertips.

Dunlop threw his arms up over his head and, after one brilliant flash of white, he too was surrounded by a corona, still blue, but this time shot through with black threads.

"Show off" Fiona said before turning to me. "A simple invisibility spell. It could have been done with a lot less show, but Arthur does love to have an audience."

I didn't understand how we could be invisible when we were lit up like fairies on a Christmas tree, but as I've said before, there was a lot about this case I didn't understand. I kept my mouth shut and followed them as they stepped onto the causeway.

This is where things start to get out of control, and I'm not even sure how much of it I believe myself. I know the story has been outlandish enough so far, but hold onto your hats, as they say in the films, you ain't seen nothing yet. I won't try to theorize over what occurred; I'll just tell the story as I think it happened and let the events speak for themselves.

When my foot hit the causeway it felt like I'd burned my bridges—there was no going back now. I looked to the other two for some reassurance, but they were both lost in concentration.

We had only gone six feet when there was a scream from the top of one of the turrets, a banshee wail that echoed around us. I stopped where I was, frozen by that eldritch scream, and immediately knew that I was not going to be able to move for a long time. The scream echoed around the cliffs, the echoes answering in a chorus of whispers.

I looked up at the house in time to see something detach itself from the roof. At first it was just another blob of darkness against the sky, but then it grew, grew and flowed as if stretching after a long sleep. It took shape quickly, spreading a pair of leathery wings as it fell before swooping upwards barely a yard from the ground and taking flight.

For a second I was back in a childhood nightmare, cowering under the evil breath of a Nazgul from Mordor as it came for me.

It wailed once more and I saw smoke coming from its distended nostrils and the red fires of hell burning brightly in its eyes as it screamed its way towards us. I had time to see a sheen of jet-black scales, scales that clashed like cold metal as the great wings beat and it swooped.

I shouted, a stream of nonsense words, but was quietened by a stern look from Fiona. I ducked at the same time as my legs gave way under me, but when I managed to look up Dunlop and Fiona were standing over me.

It went dark, and the creature came on, dived over Fiona's left shoulder, and kept going into the blackness. Fiona had a small, secretive smile on her lips.

"This is only the first barrier, used to keep away passing strangers. An illusion, that's all, nothing to frighten a big strong man like you " she said in a throaty stage whisper, not even looking at the thing that circled above us.

She was right. It swooped by overhead once more, revealing a milky white underside, before returning to its roost on the roof. The next time I looked it was just another blob on the skyline.

Dunlop took me aside and whispered sternly in my ear.

"You must control yourself. No matter what you see, or what you hear, you must keep quiet. I will tell you if there is anything to get really worried about. Okay?"

I nodded, feeling stupid and ashamed, and fell in behind them as they started moving again.

I found that if I looked out of the corner of my eye I could see the aura around me. Unlike the others, mine was green, a faint olive green that shimmered and swirled like cigarette smoke in a still room. I was so intent on watching this that I almost walked into the back of the others when they stopped.

Fiona put her hand to her lips, but she needn't have bothered—I had learned my lesson. We stood there for several seconds before I heard what had stopped them.

It came from the sea on the left-hand side, a slithering of a heavy body; the scrape as it pulled itself over the rocks on the shore. As the noise got closer I could hear something else, the rhythmic rasping of something large breathing.

Dunlop wrestled with his backpack, trying to unravel one of the straps that seemed to have got tangled at his left shoulder. He was still struggling when the thing pulled itself up onto the causeway, blocking our way to the house.

Think of a seal, then blow it up to the size of a bus. Give it a bright red weeping sore of a mouth big enough to swallow a man whole and add tiny red eyes. Then add the smell.

Its odor wafted over us and made us choke. Dunlop still hadn't got his backpack off, and as I moved forward to help him Fiona went to meet the beast.

It reared up above her, at least eight feet off the ground, towering over her slight form, the tiny red eyes staring down at her. I looked closely into those eyes, but there was no sign of intelligence, only a blind, unquestioning rage. That didn't bother Fiona. She strode forward until she was no more than three feet from the creature.

I almost screamed again, but a sharp look from Dunlop soon put paid to that. He still struggled with his backpack, but he didn't seem too concerned about his wife.

I started to move anyway, but before I had gone two yards Fiona took matters into her own hands.

She started singing, a cool, high melody, as sad as a bagpipe lament—but much more tuneful. Her aura pulsed, first deeper blue, then back to turquoise, swirling and drifting as if caught by a wind. The beast writhed in a sudden spasm, leaving strips of skin on the road surface beneath it, and the stench got worse, forcing me to gag violently. Fiona's singing got louder and her aura grew and flowed faster, growing apace with the rhythm of the song, encompassing the creature in a swirling sea of rainbow colors.

A series of spasms hit the creature and it thrashed and curled like a worm on a pin. It mewled like a lost kitten, then began to diminish. There was something wrong with my sense of perspective—it seemed to be receding away from me, but I could see that it still sat on the ground in front of Fiona. It got smaller until it was no larger than a small puppy.

It gave one final squeal, a pitiful cry of longing, before it was gone, leaving only a gray smear on the causeway.

Fiona turned back to us, just as Dunlop managed to get his backpack off. Her aura was stronger now, a deeper, richer blue with threads of gold dancing and swirling within it. But even as she spoke I could see it fading back to its previous color.

"It's a bit late now, Arthur" she said. "I don't think your services will be required." She sounded annoyed, but there was a large smile on her face.

"I thought I'd let you deal with it—it was only a small one" Dunlop said, then they hugged each other and I could see tears in his eyes.

The embrace went on for longer than I would have liked, and after several seconds I had to cough discretely.

"I'm sorry, Derek" Fiona said, prizing herself away from her husband. "It's just that it's a long time since we exercised our power—we weren't sure if we would be strong enough."

"What was it?" I asked, not really sure if I wanted to hear the answer.

"A creature from another dimension, called out of the outer regions to bar our way" Dunlop answered. "And that wasn't an illusion—you had something to worry about that time."

"Thanks for the advance warning" I muttered, not quite loud enough for him to hear. "So if it was that bad, why did you let Fiona deal with it?" I said.

"Because I have great faith in her power" he replied. "But I can't tell you any more without confusing you further." He was right there, I was confused enough already.

"Anyway. I didn't quite have this ready" he said opening his backpack and removing a one- foot long piece of untrimmed wood. It was of some dark wood that I didn't recognize, and it looked worn and polished with age and use. As soon as he touched it his aura deepened and the black threads all but disappeared. He looked five years younger.

"A wizard has to have a wand " he said by way of explanation. "Everybody knows that."

Everything had taken a comic edge and none of us seemed to be taking our situation seriously. Some form of demon had just attacked us, I had almost lost control of my bowels at the sight of a dragon, and here Dunlop was waving a bloody magic wand around.

What next? Sawing the woman in half?

"What is this—cabaret night?" I asked.

"Don't worry " Fiona replied. "I call it my hippie spell—it's always laid back." She burst into a fit of giggles, so girl-like and cute that Dunlop and I came out in sympathy.

"It helps us keep things at a distance, stops us from being overcome by fear " she said when she had recovered enough to speak. "Haven't you noticed its effect?"

"Yeah " I said, trying to sound nonchalant. "But I don't believe it's working that well. I think I need a change of underwear."

That started off the chortling again.

"Be like me, Derek " Fiona said. "Don't wear any—it saves on the laundry."

Still giggling we made our way to the gate.

We approached it slowly, and I had plenty of time to study it closely. It was fifteen feet high, a network of black iron curled and twisted into demonic faces that leered obscenely at us as we faced it. Along the top of the gate were a series of tall spikes, gleaming razor sharp in the dim light. And on top of every spike there was a head. I had to look closely to make sure that they too were cast of the same black iron. The craftsman had been brilliant—the heads were perfect, the strands of hair each individually defined, the mouths gaping in throat-tearing screams, the eyes showing pure terror.

I moved first, stepping forward and touching the lock before the other two could stop me.

The first thing I felt was pain, deep, bone wrenching pain that surged through my body like an electric shock. I tried to take my hand off the gate but it seemed to be locked in place. My hand and the cold black iron were welded into one, the pain blasting its way through my nervous system. I felt as if I was being lit up from within in black, blazing radiance. I opened my mouth, preparing to scream, but nothing came out except a low, pained moan.

My aura grew, a crawling carpet of emerald green that flowed over the gate like an over- blanket, creeping and flowing, seeking out all the hidden corners in the metal.

As it hit them, the demonic faces began to come alive, dead metal turning to thick green, warty flesh, saliva-coated tongues lolling suggestively around thin-lipped, cruel mouths. The eyes were the worst, though—they glared at me, black, cat-eye pupils shining demonically, anticipating their release.

There was a sucking sound and the shriek of tearing metal. My hand suddenly fell away from the gate as if a circuit had been broken, and the pain left me, as suddenly as it had come.

I fell to the ground in surprise; just managing to get myself back up again as four creatures pulled themselves out of the gate. The gate swung open behind them, but I didn't think we'd be going through it any time soon.

They were small, little more than three feet high, but they looked powerful, like small gorillas. Their backs were hunched so that their knuckles almost grazed the ground, reinforcing the impression of primates, but their skulls were high domes and intelligent. There was no sign of body hair, and they were completely naked, their gray skin glistening with oily sweat.

They all played with huge throbbing erections that were jutting out from their groins, organs that were much too big for the scale of their bodies. Panting with lust they made straight for Fiona.

I don't believe I have ever seen anything so obscene. They continued playing with themselves as they moved forward, and their tongues slithered redly between their thin lips, saliva dripping down their chins. Dunlop was waving the wand about, muttering under his breath, but I didn't wait.

I stepped forward and punted the nearest demon in the backside, lifting it a clear two feet off the ground. It made no sound, but it turned and was on me before I had time to react.

It climbed up my body like some crazed chimpanzee, and I found myself staring into a pair of burning eye sockets. Its tongue thrust out at me, and I couldn't close my mouth in time. My throat filled with six inches of cold flesh that tickled the back of my throat as it forced its way deeper.

I wasn't able to breathe and I felt hot vomit puddle in my stomach. I tried to prize the creature off but its grip was as strong as the iron from which it had come. Blackness crept in at the edges of my sight.

Biting down didn't work—my teeth failed to make any impression—and the flesh burrowed ever deeper, heading for my stomach. I caught a movement over to my left and Dunlop moved into sight. He waved his arms and I was suddenly blinded by a white, flashbulb blast that left a bright yellow afterimage long after it had gone.

The thing in my arms melted and flowed, becoming suddenly fluid. My nose stung as an acrid gas began to boil from the liquefying flesh before it came apart completely, falling out of my arms in a soggy, dead mass. It had left its tongue behind, a heavy load of tissue that turned to jelly in my throat. Nausea hit me hard, forcing me to my knees where I gagged and choked, vomiting my stomach contents onto the path in one hot, steaming bundle.

When I stood I saw that the demons, if that is what they had been, had all been reduced to the same state—four puddles of protoplasm that bubbled and seethed but showed no signs of being able to reform.

"Homunculi " Dunlop said as he helped me to my feet, as if that explained anything. Fiona stepped over two of the seething puddles, and the pools surged and boiled. From one a long tendril grew, larger and thicker, almost a foot long before falling back to the ground with a dull, liquid thud. I could see disgust on her face as she came towards us.

There was something different about her…something had changed. Maybe my encounter with the gate had scrambled my brains, but it took several seconds to realize what it was. Our auras had gone.

"The gate was an absorber " Fiona said. "We have lost our protections. From now on we must be more careful."

"Shit. I'm sorry " I said, and I felt it. I was out of my depth here—I didn't understand what was going on, and I would be putting the other two in danger with my stupidity.

Fiona must have seen some of those thoughts on my face.

"It's okay, Derek. The spell got us further than we thought it would, anyway. We'll just have to put up with anything they throw at us from now on."

It looked like fun time was over.

The house lay ahead of us, twin eyes scrutinizing us in unblinking hate. Dunlop suddenly looked ill again. His skin had regained its yellow pallor and he was hunched over like a whipped dog. New flecks of blood had appeared around his mouth and his eyes seemed to have sunk several inches back into his skull

Fiona put an arm around his shoulders, leading him forward, and we passed through the open gate.

Now that Fiona's spell had gone I felt the oppressive force from the house bearing down on us. Black leafless trees reached at us like charred, animated skeletons, and the door of the house waited for us like a maw leading straight to hell. By the time we had got halfway along the drive I had to help Fiona with Dunlop, and by the time we reached the door he seemed a dead weight in our arms.

Fiona asked me to put him down, gently, and we laid him on the black granite steps. I've never seen anyone look more like a corpse yet still be alive.

"The jars " he gasped, and Fiona shook her head violently, but he insisted. "It's the only way. It will give me a couple of hours—that's all I need."

I seemed to have missed something important. There were tears in her eyes as she undid the straps of the backpack. As she took the jars out they gleamed with their own sickly red light.

"It'll kill you " she said, and the tears ran down her cheeks.

"I'm dying anyway " Dunlop replied. "We knew that already. I need to be strong so that I can go the way I want to go."

She nodded, and handed him the jars.

Dunlop grasped for them eagerly, and the look in his eyes was a mixture of anticipation and self-loathing.

"Don't look " he said. "This might not be very pleasant."

Fiona and I turned away, but it wasn't enough to hide the chewing noises. I wanted to ask what was in the jars, but I was afraid of the answer. When we turned back the jars were empty and he looked marginally better. A trickle of fresh blood ran from the side of his mouth and his eyes looked dead and black.

Finally I plucked up enough courage to ask.

"What was that?" I said, but he refused to answer.

"The flesh is the life. Sometimes we have to do repellent things to achieve our goals " was all he said before turning his attention to the door.

It looked like a solid piece of oak, and I guessed it would be several inches thick, but Dunlop merely put his hand on it and muttered several words under his breath. It swung open, revealing a well-lit hall beyond.

Whoever had decorated the place had a fine sense of Gothic melodrama. Black velvet draped from every conceivable hanging place and the chandeliers were enormous, Victorian extravagances. The staircase that led away into the darkness looked to be made from black marble, and portraits of a whole army of malevolent individuals glared at us from the walls. If Durban had built this place the antiques business must pay better than I ever imagined.

It took us five minutes to find the entrance to the crypt. Dunlop had been right—the rest of the house was still and quiet—but when we found the right door we could hear the far off, muted sound of chanting. My skin crawled and goosebumps spread over my arms.

"Party time " Dunlop said. "If you get a chance, grab the amulet." He coughed and I could hear the watery gurgle in his lungs. Just as he moved towards the door he staggered and almost fell. I moved forward to help him but he brushed me away.

"Don't worry " he said, his voice almost too low to be heard. "I've got enough strength left to do what needs to be done."

"What's Plan B? What do we do if they finish the ritual?" I asked, aware that I didn't have any idea of what was happening, what I was supposed to do.

"Pray " Fiona said from behind me as she brushed past and was the first to go down into the crypt. Dunlop followed her, leaving me bringing up the rear.

Just as we started down the chanting from below stopped and silence descended, leaving us to the quiet, heavy dark that loomed around us.

The walls were built of large blocks of sandstone. I had visited several Neolithic tombs, in Carnac, in Orkney and on Salisbury Plain. This gave the same sense of age, of a time long past. What I hadn't expected, what was completely different, was the overwhelming feeling that this place was in use. The walls ran damp and there was a salt tang in the air, but there was no sign of moss or lichen on the walls—only the damp glistening stone and the carvings.

I didn't have time to study them, but I could see that they didn't fit with any system I'd ever heard of. Doug might have made sense of them, but he wasn't here. The thought of my friend's fate gave me added impetus, and I walked faster down the steps.

The path kept going down, deeper and deeper, and the air was getting colder and damper. At first the light from the hall above dimly lighted the way, but the path curved and we were soon in darkness. I groped my way along the walls, led on by the liquid breathing from Dunlop, and tried not to think of tentacled monstrosities creeping along in the darkness behind us.

I judged that we must be under the sea by now, and the thought of all that water above added an extra worry line to my already furrowed brow. At least the passage hadn't diverged. Not yet, anyhow.

I started to wonder how far we had to go when I heard the noise. It was far off and sounded like the morning cry of a gull, but the noise grated on my nerves and sent a cold shiver down my spine.

"Tukeli li. Tukeli li."

It pounded in my head like a chant. I was so busy listening that I stumbled when my foot didn't meet the expected step and the path leveled out.

A soft hand covered my mouth, and I smelled Fiona's perfume as she led me away from the entrance. My eyes started to acclimatize themselves to the room, and I could see that it wasn't quite pitch dark.

We were in a small chamber, cut off from another room beyond by a heavy black curtain. Dunlop was peering through a small gap. He turned and motioned for us to follow as he slipped through to a large, candlelit chamber, some thirty feet in diameter. There were twelve hooded figures at the far end, standing in front of some sort of altar, all with their backs to us. Dunlop led us around a column of rock from behind which we were able to watch the proceedings.

It looked like we had arrived just in time. A tall figure I recognized as Durban moved forward and placed the amulet on the altar. I made a move, but was pulled back by Fiona. "Not yet " she mouthed silently, keeping a tight grip on my arm.

Durban prostrated himself in front of the altar, and the group began to chant. I couldn't be sure, but it sounded like the same one they had used the previous night, its dissonance and slightly off-tune harmonics shaking the walls around us, making the room feel even colder than it already was.

Once more the old woman stepped forward, and the song started again. I guessed we were about to see the return of the tentacled creature.

I was proved right several seconds later when the fetid odor spread throughout the chamber and there was a rippling in the air above the altar.

This time it came through already changed, the pumpkin head forcing itself into existence first, tearing a rapidly growing hole in space, like a monstrous birthing. The air in the chamber had become thick and cloying, and the echoes of the chanting rang all around us.

And there seemed to be an answering from beyond the hole being made by the thing—high- pitched piping like some crazed flute player in the unimaginable distance.

The tentacled head kept coming, the head at least five feet across and the tentacles now nearly as thick as my wrist where they met the head. It pushed the final piece of its bulk through, pulling the torso and legs through behind it, and lay on the altar, head pulsing in time with the chanting.

The hole in space stayed open above it, a black chasm through which a chill wind whistled, bringing a thin coating of frost to the altar. The flute was still there, closer now, and a deep, bass drumming had joined it, a primitive throbbing that jerked my nerves and made me want to throw off my clothes and dance.

I had actually begun to move forward when Dunlop turned me towards him. He touched me between the eyes with his stick of wood and the compulsion left me as suddenly as it had come. I could still hear the drumming, it still beat heavy in my head, but I no longer wished to obey it. On the altar two of the tentacles swayed above the bulbous head, then brought themselves down onto the amulet. As they touched it there was a burst of green light, and as they lifted it up towards the black hole in reality the chanting changed, becoming louder and more guttural.

The black hole began to grow, ripping its way open in the air with a tearing scream, and the green light oozed through to the other side, travelling against the flow of the wind. The reedy piping got louder, until I felt that my eardrums were going to burst, and that was when Dunlop made his move.

He moved past me like a bat out of hell, screaming at the top of his lungs, blue lancing flame shooting from the piece of wood in his hand. He was aiming straight for the thing on the altar, and it didn't look like anything would stop him.

Then all hell broke loose.

Fiona began to sing, softly at first but rapidly rising to a crescendo, drowning out the piping. The cowled figures scattered before Dunlop's attack, but the pumpkin head never moved, seemingly soaking up the blue flame.

I felt a hand push me in the back. "Help him!" Fiona said before returning to her song, and I staggered, off balance, into the robed group. I was among them before they realized it, and I got halfway towards Dunlop before they thought of stopping me.

A large figure blocked my path. I shoved him to one side, but he grabbed my arm and partly turned me around. I threw a punch, but only succeeded in dislodging the cowl, which fell back, revealing Durban's craggy face. I struggled to regain my balance when his fist slammed into my jaw, knocking me backward towards the left-hand side of the altar. The blow wasn't hard, but it was enough to make me lose my balance again. As I fell I heard a tearing in the air behind me. I put my hand out to steady myself and hit the edge of the altar. Immediately a tentacle made a grab for my wrist. I just managed to pull my hand away but was unable to retain balance. There was a further tearing noise, like a piece of paper being slowly ripped.

A wind rose, first tugging gently, but as I fell backwards it turned into a raging, roaring gale. The blackness sucked me in like a fly into a vacuum cleaner.

I think I screamed but the wind in my ears drowned out all other noise. I could see only inky blackness as I fell and fell and fell, the darkness tugging at me, the wind ruffling my hair.

My muscles tensed, expecting a landing, ready for impact, but the wind began to die down. It felt like I was slowing. I waved my arms around my head, but could feel nothing except the thick blackness. The air was heavy, almost the consistency of water, but I could still breathe, as I slowed even further. Finally, I stopped, floated in darkness, no idea of up or down

I rolled over onto my back, and there, an unimaginable distance away, was a small blue light, twinkling like a star.

From somewhere far beneath I could hear the distant sound of manic piping, but it sounded further away that it had when I was in the chamber. Apart from that there was no other noise, no other light. The air moved sluggishly around me, tasteless and odorless. I almost felt calm.

I discovered that I could propel myself by using swimming actions and began to make my way towards the light, slowly at first, but ever accelerating as my body got into the rhythm of the actions.

It was heavy going and at first I didn't seem to be making much headway, but then the light seemed to pulse brighter, the hole growing, and I began to move even faster towards it. In the distance I could hear Fiona singing, her voice still strong, still pure, leading me back to the light.

Then, from the corner of my eye, I caught a flicker of light, like a stray moonbeam in a cloudy sky. And I heard it, the soft cry, the voice I had heard in my dreams.

"Help me " it said, and I had no doubt that it came from Doug. "Help me!" it shouted again, and this time the voice rose to a scream, a scream full of pain and despair. I had one last, longing, look at the blue dancing light before turning away towards the sound of my friend.

The going got tough, like swimming through treacle, but I was getting there, even though it was now like swimming through thick oil. The piping was getting noticeably louder and more frantic as I got closer, and the drums beat louder, pounding into my head and reverberating in my chest cavity until my heart was beating along in time.

Doug lay in a pool of light, curled up into a fetal ball, hugging his knees so hard that I could see the whiteness at his knuckles. I quickly checked his body for punctures, but there was only one obvious wound—a weeping hole in his cheek.

There was something else there, though, very close to him, a deeper cloud of blackness that seemed to be the source of the piping, but I didn't have time to study it further—my only thought was for Doug.

He still had his back to me. I pulled myself forward and touched his arm. His body unfolded and he turned to face me, already screaming.

"Help me!"

I had a sudden flash of my dream, of the tentacles bursting from him, but his eyes looked so full of fear and panic that I was unable to refuse. I took his hand, pulling him towards me, trying not to look at the festering hole in his cheek. He grabbed me, tight, and hugged me so hard that I began to worry about broken ribs. Suddenly I heard Fiona's singing again, and it got colder, so cold that small ice crystals formed in the air around us.

The piping rose in intensity and I sensed a movement behind me, at the same time noticing that the blue star seemed to be speeding towards us, growing as it came. There was a crackling, and I could feel static run over my body, and my hair stood on end. I turned, and saw that the blackness behind me had also grown and expanded. Things moved in it, black amorphous shapes that struggled and pushed as if against a plastic membrane, trying to break through.

Suddenly we were bathed in blue, crackling light, and space ripped around us as the two holes converged and met. There was a blinding flash and when my eyes adjusted we were lying beneath the altar, back in the chamber.

I looked up, and could not believe what I saw.

Above me Dunlop was held in the tentacles of the pumpkin head, five of them around his waist alone, a multitude of small puncture marks covering his body, blood pulsing slowly from each of them. But the creature wasn't getting it all its own way. Four tentacles lay limp against the head, their ends looking oddly twisted and charred.

Dazzling blue flame shot from the wand in his hand and the smell of charred flesh rose from the red, bulbous head. The history of Dunlop's attack was there—the head was furrowed by four canyons of burnt, steaming flesh, the smell of cooking meat heavy in the air.

Dunlop tried to reach the amulet that was still being held above the head, but now by only one tentacle.

I raised my eyes to the tentacle, and was almost riven through in shock. Beyond the amulet the ceiling was a mass of writhing blackness.

Imagine a black plastic bin bag filled with writhing snakes, and you'll have some idea of what I saw. Some idea, but nothing could really describe the overwhelming sense of dread I felt as I looked at it.

The veil was thin and stretched in places—whatever was behind striving hard to break through, it didn't look like it would be too long before it succeeded.

Somewhere behind me Fiona still sang, but I couldn't turn to look, blocked by Doug who lay whimpering in my arms. I moved sideways, lowering him gently to the floor, and tried to stand. Dunlop shouted at me.

"Derek!"

His voice was strained, and I couldn't even begin to imagine the kind of pain he must have been in, but he was still lucid, and he still fought.

I looked up. Several of the tentacles burrowed into his body, the blood gushing in torrents at his waist and shoulders. But there was little trace of pain in his voice as he spoke again.

"Get Fiona out of here! And don't take no for an answer!"

That was all he had time for. By speaking to me he had given the tentacles an opening, and one of them attached itself to his left hand, chewing its way through fingers, spattering fine droplets of blood onto my face.

I got to my feet and looked around. Durban lay on the ground, not six feet from me, dead eyes staring roofward. His hand clutched at his chest, at a gaping, smoking hole. I guessed that he had got in Dunlop's way.

There was no sign of the rest of the coven. Fiona stood where I had left her. She still sang strongly, but tears glistened in her eyes and ran unfettered down her cheeks as she watched what happened to her husband.

At my feet Doug tried to get up, his eyes wild and deranged as he stared around the room. There was madness in his eyes, and a terrible fear. He clawed at me as I helped him to his feet, clinging to me as the only recognizable thing in the hell that his life had become.

"Get out of here!" I shouted at him, twice before he understood me. He nodded his head as I pushed him away, directing him towards the exit before heading for Fiona.

"Come on!" I shouted, trying to make myself heard above the cacophony of fluting that echoed through the chamber. I grabbed her by the shoulders but she shrugged me off easily.

"We've got to get away from here. It's over " I said, gently, but with some fervor. I was as eager as Doug to get as far away from this place as possible. She shook her head without breaking her singing and began to move towards the altar. I really had no choice but to follow her, but I was stopped in my tracks by the sight that met me when I turned.

Two more tentacles pierced Dunlop's body, and thick red blood poured in a river from his mouth. At first I feared he was already dead, but his eyes were still alive as he lifted the wand above his head. There was another blinding flash of blue light and the amulet fell to the ground, a writhing piece of tentacle still attached.

At the same moment there was a rending in the blackness. I had a glimpse of a purple sky above as a split appeared in the membrane.

I can't describe some of the things I saw there—they seemed to defy the eye, to melt and flow like molten mercury. There was something solid amid the fluidity—a leathery, barrel- shaped body with a five-pointed star where its head should be and huge, gossamer, veined wings.

Then the horde behind the veil parted and something huge and black began to make its way forward. I have an impression of tentacles of an immense size, but my memory of the true shape of the creature has gone, burned for the sake of my sanity. I can only say that it was huge, it was old, and it was hell-bent on coming through.

Fiona stood in front of the altar. I shouted at her, but she ignored me and bent to the floor. She picked up the amulet. It pulsed a sickly green in her hands.

Above her Dunlop still fired great gouts of flame at the creature that held him, but the flame no longer held its dazzling blue quality, and, although he still damaged the creature, the wounds he inflicted were no longer as deep or as penetrating.

Fiona held the amulet at arm's length, oblivious to the tentacle that hit her in the midriff and immediately began to burrow.

She looked at her husband, and I caught the slow nod of his head and the spreading smile on his face as she drew her arm back and the amulet sailed through the air. Despite the efforts of three tentacles to catch it, it disappeared into the gulf beyond the rift.

She turned to me, tentacles now writhing over her torso, and said just one word before reaching out to clasp her husband's hand.

"Go " she said. I moved towards them but was too late. The pumpkin head writhed and all the tentacles screamed in a chorus.

There was a flash, a blinding explosion that seared through my brain, knocking me almost senseless to the floor, a floor that shook and bucked as if in the throes of some diabolic birthing.

Dunlop lay limp in the creature's grasp, but Fiona was still alive, only just. She leaned forward to the creature's great head and thrust her hands into it, passing through the flesh as if it were plasticine. She jerked her hands, just once, and the creature screamed, a roar that shook the walls and dislodged small pieces of dust to hang in the air.

The veil bulged, swollen like a balloon filled with water, then burst in an explosion of rainbow light that forced me to close my eyes again. And when I opened them, Fiona, Dunlop and the creature were gone and there was no sign of the rift in space. I was left alone in silence, with Durban's dead body and the body of an ancient Arab lying across the altar, a body that was decomposing even as I watched.

Pieces of earth fell into the chamber as a jagged crack ran across the ceiling. I just managed to make it to the stairway before the roof collapsed in a flurry of rubble and masonry. I fled up the stairs as the walls swayed and the roof threatened to come down on me.

Doug lay in the hallway. At first I thought he was dead, and I panicked, shaking him hard and cradling him to my chest.

It took me several seconds to realize that he was still breathing. I hoisted him over my shoulder in a fireman's carry, almost bent double by his weight, and got out of the house as quickly as I could. The structure fell down around me and the floor heaved like the deck of a ship. I made it out of the door and into the garden, but I don't remember how.

I laid Doug down on the grass and turned back, in time to see the eyes of the house flare redly for one last time before collapsing in on itself in a storm of smoke, burying the crypt and all who laid in it under several hundred tons of stone.

And that's the end of it.

I visit Doug every week, and he's coming along fine, but there is still fear down deep in his eyes, and he sleeps with the light on.

As for me, I went back to the newspaper business.

The police never bothered me about Stan and Ollie. I reported finding the bodies— anonymously, of course—and just happened to mention how close they were to Durban's house. That must have been enough for the powers that be. The story never made the papers—I'm not sure anyone would have found it believable anyway.

The only evidence of anything untoward came in the obituary—Durban's, Fiona's and Dunlop's appeared on the same day, all having died 'suddenly, and at home'. I visited their graves once, but there was no sense of any power there—how could there be, when their bodies are somewhere beyond this earth?

At least being back on the paper gives me the chance to check on any news of Arkham House. I shift pieces of paper, I interview local councilors, and I keep my eyes open for stories concerning lost cats.

I often find myself daydreaming of being back in my office above Byres Road, waiting for Fiona Dunlop to drop in, but all in all I'm contented—sometimes boredom is a much sought after condition.

At nights I dream, dreams in which something huge and black and monstrous tries to break through a veil, a veil that gets thinner and thinner. And every night I wake up screaming.

But that's not quite the end of it. I haven't yet come to the reason I'm writing this story when it would have been better to forget it completely.

I found it in the Times three days ago—and I can't get it out of my mind. It was in the description of items coming up for sale at Sotheby's.

Lot 29 -- The Johnson Amulet. Long feared lost, newly returned to the market, this is one of the most interesting archaeological artifacts to come to our attention for a long time. Private sale, bidding will start at £400 000.

About the Author

William Meikle is a Scottish writer with more than twelve novels published in the genre press and over 200 short story credits in thirteen countries.

He is the author of the ongoing Midnight Eye series among others, and his work appears in a number of professional anthologies. His ebook THE INVASION has been as high as #2 in the Kindle SF and Kindle Horror charts.

He lives in a remote corner of Newfoundland with ice-bergs, whales and bald eagles for company. In the winters he gets warm vicariously through the lives of others in cyberspace, so check him out at www.williammeikle.com.

Made in the USA
Las Vegas, NV
02 January 2022

40038971R00146